VICIOUS
VI CARTER

WARNING

This book is a dark romance. This book contains scenes that may be triggering to some readers and should be read by those only 18 or older.

NEWSLETTER

Join my newsletter and never miss a new release or giveaway by scanning the QR code below:

CHAPTER ONE

O'REAGAN
AN CHLANN

SHANE

"**P**ass me the shovel." I gesture to Finn as I stare into the shallow grave. The smell of decay rises up to greet us. Recent rainfall has caused the grave to sink in further. Coming here tonight was the right thing to do. If we left it any longer, the body would be exposed.

"I can't do this."

"You will do this." I glare at Finn to drive my words home, and he's shaking his head like he has options.

Sinking to his hunkers, he runs both hands down his face, like he can erase what he's seeing. "That's Siobhan's aunt."

His eyes are glued to the grave. Regret at bringing him here is starting to slowly raise its head. Finn and Darragh, who are the youngest of us brothers, have it way too easy. They were born with silver spoons in their mouths. So right now, I just want to dirty Finn's hands a little bit. The idea is giving me far too much joy.

"I don't really care who it is. Now pass me the shovel."

Finn gets up and takes both shovels that lean against the boot of my Mercedes. His steps are careful across the bog. The land we purchased was deliberate. A bog is ideal for what we're currently doing.

The lights from my car shine on the ground and stop just at the grave. The sun is nearly gone, and soon, the car will be our only source of light, so I want this done before that happens. Once the shovel is in my hand, I start to dig. Finn stands still, leaning against his shovel, watching me.

"Finn," I warn, and he starts to dig. It doesn't take us long before all the clay is off the body. Wildlife have gotten to her. We wrapped her in plastic, but her head hangs out, her neck twisted at an awkward angle. Finn turns away and gags repeatedly. His early dinner splashes on the mud and on his shoes.

"You'll take off your shoes before you get back into my car," I warn him. Holding my breath, I pull the body fully out of the grave. We need to dig deeper. We buried her in a panic in a shallow grave.

"You're heartless." Finn wipes his mouth with the back of his hand.

"Who was the one who bashed her head in?" I question, and his eyes shift away from me. "You had one job, Finn—to keep an eye on Darragh. But you couldn't do that could you?"

His head snaps up, his eyes bulging. "I'm not his fucking babysitter."

"That's exactly what you are," I remind him. "If you hadn't been lying with that girl, none of this would have happened."

"Shane, don't bring her into this." He's taking a step toward me. I'm not threatened by him. My shovel sinks into the wet ground easily, and I start digging, ending our pointless conversation.

We work in silence and once the grave is deep enough, I dump the body in. Finn looks away in horror, and I suppress a smile.

"Jesus. We should say a prayer."

Prayer? Like that will bring her back. I leave Finn to say his prayers. The heavy plastic that I pull off the dead animal releases a smell and a swarm of flies. I turn my head to the left to avoid a mouthful of them.

"Finn," I call. His low words cease, and he tuts before he joins me. I've already tied ropes around the front of the cow's legs. It's an odd-colored cow. Black, white, and red—a mixed breed. Not that it matters. I pick one of the ropes up and hand the other to Finn. He's gawking at me, and I exhale loudly.

"We use the cow to cover the body, so if anyone digs, they hit the cow first and don't bother digging any further," I tell him and start pulling. He doesn't say anything but pulls too. It's heavier than I expected, but we manage to get the cow into the grave. We push it in on top of the body, and the impact is loud.

"Did you hear something break?" I ask Finn, and his eyes narrow.

"Are you fucking joking?" He has no sense of humor.

We finish off by covering the body with clay just as the sun sets. I close the boot once everything is cleaned up and stop Finn from climbing into my car.

"Remove your shoes." I didn't forget him retching on them. He shakes his head but kicks them off. They join the rest of the stuff in the boot.

"I need my bed," Finn says, closing his eyes and leaning back against the headrest. The first pitter-patter of rain hits the windshield as I start the car.

Leaving the bog, I then drive home to the Whitewood house.

CHAPTER TWO

O'REAGAN
AN CHLANN

SHANE

My father glances up from his desk as I close the double doors behind me. Dark circles under his eyes, along with his disheveled appearance, make me want to tell him to go to bed. He's loosened his tie and opened the top button of his shirt.

After his declaration that he knew where Connor was, I had to talk to him. I don't like finding things out along with the others; I thought I was more privileged than them. He asked me to get Connor, his request taking the sting out of it, but not enough for me to let it go.

"How long have you known where Connor is?" I ask. His rising hand, holding the letter opener, cuts me off. A half-opened white envelope is the only thing on his desk.

"I don't." He shakes his head while he speaks, then puts down the letter opener. "I had eyes on him until last week."

The bookcase that fills the wall behind his desk is a display of colors—mostly browns, reds, and greens. I've always hated the smell and general appearance of the books. As I sit down, I try to make sense of what my father is saying.

"So why only send me now? Why not a week ago when he went missing?" Irritation pours over my words, and I don't try to lessen it.

Connor is a valuable source to our family. He isn't exactly family, but we need him. He maintains a balance that we can't seem to find without him. We try, but things never sit right when he's gone.

"I thought maybe he was having an off day. But a day turned into a few. I've recently gotten word that he's crossed the border." Father rubs between his eyes, and I find myself picking up his letter opener and standing it up on the desk.

This isn't good. Crossing into the north isn't allowed; it's declared by a different group. One we don't interfere with. They claim to be the real Republican Army. So, we keep far away.

"Why would he do that?" I ask while sitting back and taking the letter opener with me. It's not sharp; I stick it against my thumb and spin it.

"I'm not sure. But I want you to find out why, and I want you to bring him back." Father holds out his hand, and I tap the letter opener against my palm.

I want him to answer another question before he dismisses me. "Did you ring Tom and have it confirmed?"

His eyes narrow at my question, and his jaw clenches. He holds out his hand again, and I give him what he wants. Once he has it, he finishes opening the letter.

"Of course I did. He's seen and heard nothing." My father won't meet my eye, and I question what he's holding back.

I sit back in the chair and twist the silver band on my thumb in circles. "And you believe him?" I quiz.

I don't get an answer. Loud commotion in the hall has both of us standing up and leaving the study. Finn, Darragh, and our stepsister, Una, are in the hall. My eyes snap to Liam. He stands to the side, still wearing a full suit as he observes Darragh, who is drunk, and Finn, who is the only one trying to control the situation.

My attention is drawn back to Una. She's always had an ability to capture my attention. Her fiery red hair hangs dark and limp down her back. She looks like she just stepped out of the ocean. A pool of water is gathering around her, but she doesn't seem aware of it. Her cream top is see-through, and a bright pink bra is visible and full.

"Get me some towels," Finn barks at Darragh. Darragh doesn't move. He stands still and laughs at Una. He's pointing at her like he's five. I turn as I hear receding footsteps behind me to find Father leaving.

"Finn, take care of this," he calls over his shoulder. Finn's head snaps up, and he looks ready to lose it.

I don't try to defuse the situation. Instead, I stand and observe to see what will happen. Finn doesn't ask me or Liam to help. Maybe he knows we won't.

Once again, Una captures my attention as she pulls a plump lip between her teeth and bites it. A laugh leaves her mouth, and she opens her eyes. They still manage to hold me in awe—one blue, the other green.

I've never seen anyone like Una. Her eyes suit her. She is two very different people. She's unpredictable, and I often think that's why I'm drawn to her. Right now, she holds out her arms and starts to twirl.

"Una, stop it." Finn tries to pull her hands down, but she keeps spinning, and Darragh joins her. That's when I decide I've seen enough. I cast a quick glance over to the spot where Liam stood, but it's empty.

As I enter the garage, I don't have to flick on the lights; they're already on. Liam waits for me by my car. "We need to take a drive."

I don't question him and slide into my Audi as he gets into the passenger seat. The garage door opens as I back out.

"You look at Father differently," he says.

"What are you talking about?" I take a left out onto the road.

"Just an observation," he says, and when I peek at Liam, he's staring at me with brown eyes that are almost black. They're the same eyes I see in the mirror.

"Don't try to analyze me. Stick with analyzing Finn and Darragh," I tell him.

"Is this topic making you uncomfortable, brother?" Liam is enjoying himself. He likes to torture me in the smallest ways. The ways I don't like.

"Of course not, *brother*," I answer as my hands grip the steering wheel.

"Take a left at the next crossroads," Liam informs me, no teasing in his voice now.

"He's different," I say, and at once, I hate that I said it. Liam is watching me again.

"How so?" To anyone else, his voice doesn't rise and fall. It's almost monotone. But listening to him for so long, I can hear that tilt in his words. It happens when he's truly curious.

"I'm not sure. I think he's hiding something." I take a left at the crossroads as he instructed.

"What were you talking about in the study?"

I laugh. I can't help it. This level of curiosity is unusual for Liam.

"Indulge me." His lips lift slightly as he speaks. "Take a right at the next crossroads," he adds.

"If you told me where we were going, it would make this easier. Is it Kells?" I question.

"It doesn't matter. Now tell me what you were talking about."

I grip the steering wheel again at his demand. "It was about Connor. He doesn't really know where he is." This conversation is annoying me. I glance at Liam, and he sits back, not facing me any longer. He stares out the window.

"To the land."

I stop at the crossroads and take a right back toward Nobber. "You've just taken us in a full circle," I say, but Liam has gone quiet. I turn up the music as I put my foot down and drive at a hundred and twenty kilometers an hour the rest of the way. We reach the land fifteen minutes later. I pull up along the lane and lower the music.

"She's been declared missing," Liam says, looking out onto the land.

My stomach tightens, but I knew this would happen. "But nothing is pointing at us?" I question, and Liam gives me a quick glance before he starts fixing his cuffs, then his collar—things that don't need to be fixed.

"No, but I have a bad feeling. I want to dig her up."

"Liam, it's been weeks," I remind him. An old moldy body after a few days isn't something I want to dig up.

"We didn't go deep enough." We buried her late at night, and he was right, we hadn't gone deep enough. It was something that had bothered me too.

"I went back a while later. I buried her deeper." Surprise is visible on Liam's face. It's small, but his eyebrows lift slightly. To anyone else, he would seem emotionless.

"I covered her with the carcass of a cow," I add.

"You did it all by yourself?"

I smile at his question and pull out away from the land. "No, I had help." It wasn't the nicest thing I've ever done, getting Finn to help me move his girlfriend's aunt's body, but it was fun.

"I got Finn to help me." I can see the wheels turning in Liam's head.

"You should have left him alone," he says, and I glance at him.

"Why? Because him being upset just might upset poor little Darragh?" I hate how soft Liam is when it comes to Darragh. I don't have a clue why. If I had a choice, I would have both Darragh and Finn out of the family business. They're both weak and cause more problems than we need.

"No, Shane. You did it with emotion, and that is stupid."

"He's a little spoilt prick. He never has to do anything. He has it easy. I just wanted to get his hands a little dirty." I'm smiling again. I can't help it. It was satisfying to see him squirm and panic.

"His hands are dirty now," Liam says, and I hate how he sounds. It's like he's telling me it will come back and bite me in the ass. I don't care.

I drop Liam off at home. He says no more about Finn or the body, and I pull away from the house before anyone else comes out. This time, I blare the music and let it pound into my head. It's senseless music, the type you can get lost in. I lose myself for the next twenty minutes as I make my way to the last place Connor was seen.

I park in a gravel car park that holds two cars and make my way into the stone building. A few men are drinking while watching a show about darts. They study me as I enter, and I let them.

My clothes speak of wealth and good taste. I know how I look. Everything is tailor-made. The barman is wiping the same spot he has been since I entered. I don't sit, but I stop at the bar.

"I'm looking for my brother," I say, and he snaps his head up at me and then at the picture I have of Connor. It's a few years old, but I can't imagine he's changed too much in the last two years.

Recognition lights up in the barman's eyes. "Connor is your brother?" He sounds unsure, and I don't blame him.

"Half brother. I'm the good-looking one." I flash a quick smile to add to my joke, and it puts him at ease. I ask my questions, and he tells me that Connor was a good tenant, and he always paid his rent on time.

"Would it be possible to see where he was staying?" I ask.

"Sure. Just give me a minute." I don't even have to wait the full minute before I'm taken upstairs, and he leads me into a small, poky, and unlivable space. I'm not sure what I thought I would find here. But a single bed with a double-doored wardrobe is all that greets me. I leave with no leads as to where Connor is.

It's getting late, so I call it a night. The house is quiet when I return home. A drink is what I need. The hallway is lit by lights that hang over large paintings. Rugs under my feet make my footsteps silent. Dark wood gives the large hallway a warmth it shouldn't hold for its sheer size. I enter the bar and find my father smoking a cigar, sitting on a Queen Ann chair with his eyes closed.

"Any luck?" he asks, not opening his eyes, and I'm curious about how he knows it's me. I pour two whiskeys, and he opens his eyes when I place his glass on the table beside him, the one that holds a large crystal ashtray.

"No, none." I take a deep drink before putting the glass on the table beside the couch I sit down on. Air brushes my skin as I roll up my sleeves. I had a tattoo done, and the skin is still fragile.

A large blank band that goes the full way around my arm joins the other eight. The tattoo starts at my elbow and reaches my wrist. Nine bands—one for each life I've taken.

My father's eyes linger on my tattoo. It's something we never speak of, but it's my way of remembering every life I ended. It's never easy to take a life, but sometimes it's a matter of theirs or mine. Or my family's.

"Una is asleep. I couldn't get a coherent word out of her." Father sounds tired again.

"Send her home." Even as I say it, I know it's a lie. I don't want her to leave. But this place has a way of twisting people, and she isn't someone I want to see hurt.

"I'll discuss that with her in the morning. But while she's here, I expect you to keep an eye on her."

I nod into my glass; I knew I would be asked. He might give Finn responsibility, but really, it's me and Liam he trusts, and Liam makes most females uncomfortable.

"Of course," I tell him before emptying my glass.

We say good night as I leave the bar. He's still smoking his cigar, and puffs of smoke swirl above his head.

A part of me says to take the left once I reach the top of the stairs, but I take the right. I should turn back, but I don't. Instead, I stand outside the room that is Una's. She never declared it, but it's a room we all know as hers, even if she doesn't. I open the door and step in.

She's lost in the four-poster bed. Her hair has dried out, and it fans around her head like a burning sun. The covers are to her neck and tucked in around her body. She's afraid of the dark. She thinks if her legs or arms aren't tucked under the quilt, something will grab her.

I smile. That's what she told me when we were kids. But she has always tucked the blanket tightly around her, even as I watched her grow from a girl into a woman. I relax as I focus on her sleeping form. This is something *I've* always done—snuck into her room and watched her sleep. It helps me. I stay for until she stirs. She's never caught me in her room before. I leave, not wanting to make this the first time.

CHAPTER THREE

O'REAGAN
AN CHLANN

UNA

I stretch out my arms and legs, and still, my legs don't dangle out of the bed like they would at home. A strangled scream is pulled from my mouth as I open my eyes. Darragh is sitting on the side of my bed, dressed and freshly washed. His blond hair is combed back. The red collared T-shirt is pressed and sits perfectly on his lean frame.

"My God, Darragh, you nearly gave me a heart attack." I sit up and clutch the quilt to my chest. His blue eyes disappear as he starts to laugh.

"What are you doing in my room?" I'm still angry, as my heart hasn't returned to its normal rhythm.

"Do you know you talk in your sleep?" Darragh tilts his head, his eyes filled with devilment.

I narrow my eyes at him and loosen my death grip on the quilt. "No, I don't," I reply and his smirk grows.

"How would you know? You were asleep."

An excellent question, just one I wasn't going to give him an answer to. "What are you doing in my room?" I ask again as I lie down. My headache returns with a vengeance. "How much did I drink last night?" I cover my eyes with my arm. His laughter isn't doing my head any good.

"You jumped into the lake."

I sit up again as snippets come back, and I let out a groan. I had; I remember now. Partying down at the lake. Darragh had dared me. "We are so stupid," I tell him, and he grins as he gets off my bed.

"Correction—you are stupid. I didn't jump in. I dared you to jump in, not thinking you would actually do it." He walks around the bed and sits on the other side. "I had to send Fran in to get you."

I cover my burning face. I remember a boy with long blond hair pulling me from the lake. He pulled me on shore. I could have drowned if not for him.

"Why didn't you rescue me?" I ask, observing him through my fingers.

"The jumper I was wearing was brand new. So…"

"Get out of my room." I'm pissed at Darragh again. Not about him not jumping into the lake to rescue me. Two drunken people in the lake wouldn't have been the best idea. Especially Darragh and me. But the fact that he picked a jumper over me—yeah, that stung.

"Are you staying with us?" Darragh asks, backing out of my room. He doesn't sound offended at me asking him to leave the room.

"I'm not sure," I tell him honestly. I need to talk to Michael first.

"Well, if you are, I have a party we can go to." He grins as he closes my door, not waiting for an answer. Darragh knows how to party hard. I'm not sure my head is up to it.

After a shower, I get dressed. I came with nothing but had left some clothes here last summer. Jeans and a moss green jumper are the best I can pull out of the bundle.

I find Michael in the kitchen. Something tells me he's been waiting for me.

"It's great to have you home." His arms are outstretched, and I can't stop the smile that spreads across my face as I walk into his arms. His warmth envelops me as his arms circle around me.

Just like that, I'm a little girl again. Michael has always had the ability to make me forget the bad.

"But what's brought you here?" he asks before planting a kiss on my head. I want to stick out my bottom lip and ask him to skip this part, but I know we can't. Michael gets me a coffee as I push my drying curls out of my eyes and sit at the breakfast bar.

"I needed to get away," I answer as he pushes a coffee into my hands.

"You want me to have a chat?"

I smile and pat his hand. "Nope, I already had words with her." I shrug as I take a drink of coffee.

Michael takes a drink of his own coffee before setting down the mug and fixing his tie, which is slightly crooked. "You can stay here as long as you want."

Relief bubbles through me. I never thought he would throw me out, but hearing him say I could stay relaxes me. He stands again and comes around to me. Brushing curls off my forehead, he gives me a kiss. "But there is a condition, my dear."

I raise both eyebrows as I wait for Michael to tell me. I can see a spark of mischief in his eyes.

"You have to work. I will get Shane to give you a job." Michael releases me and puts on his suit jacket.

The thought of working with Shane does funny things to my stomach. I've always crushed on him, but he's always looked at me like I'm repulsive. A part of me kind of gets it. My hair and eyes don't exactly make dating easy. I've been called every variation of red, and not in a pleasant way. And my eyes get me a lot of attention, but I've been called a freak because they are different colors.

"It won't be hard, Una." Michael has taken my internal struggle as a problem with him getting me to work. I shake my head.

"No, that's fine. Sorry, I was miles away." I push a smile forward, and Michael nods.

"Okay, I'm off to work," he tells me as he takes his coffee down to his office.

After the conversation with Michael, my mind moves to my mother. She was angry the last time we spoke. I was studying accountancy, following in her footsteps, and I could do it. But I found myself getting bored. I did it because she wanted me to. I had one final year, and I knew finishing made sense, but I had enough of silence and numbers. Her life wasn't for me.

I leave the kitchen with a granola bar. Mary would fix me breakfast if I wanted, but right now, I want the fresh air. I've spent way too much time indoors, and I hate it.

It's foggy this morning but warm, so I don't need a jacket. I can hear the horses in the stables as I walk along the pass. The boys have no idea just how lucky they are living here.

Stephen, one of the stable masters, comes into view. His navy boiler suit covers him as he shovels out the stables.

"Good morning, Stephen." I nearly give the man a heart attack and laugh.

He smiles. "Una, you're back."

I shrug. "Yeah, I think so." His brown peaky cap covers his balding head. He's been here as long as I can remember.

"How is she?" I ask as I make my way to the third stable.

"She's good. Her form has been off lately," he tells me as he leans the shovel against the stables and walks down to me. I stop outside my mare's door, and there's that sudden rush of sadness and happiness at seeing her. She moves back away from me, dancing slightly.

"I've had a hoof trimmer here. Her shoes are fine." I'm nodding as I open the door. But she's unsteady while moving deeper into her stable.

"How long has she been like this?" I ask as he closes the gate after me.

"A few days."

"Could she be pregnant?" I hold out my hand, and when my fingers meet her hair, she settles, allowing me to rub her side.

When Stephen doesn't answer me, I glance at him, and he's smiling. "You're the first who's been able to touch her." At his words, I lean my face into her and inhale the warm air that rises from her coat.

"We checked, but it could be too early to tell if she's pregnant. But it's possible."

I stay with her for a while, just rubbing her, and she lets me. I never named her. Shane bought the horse for me on my sixteenth birthday. I thought if I referred to her as 'her' or 'the horse' that I would never get attached. I was wrong.

It's a while later that I leave. The cold and hunger drive me back inside, and I smile when I see Mary in the kitchen. She's taking cookies out of the oven. I knock on the door, not wanting to frighten her. She has a weak heart already.

"Hi, Mary," I say. Her eyes widen, and her eyebrows rise. "Una. You are more beautiful each time I see you." She's always been too kind to me. Before she pulls me into a hug, she places the cookie tray on the counter. "Are you staying long?" She asks the same question that everyone has asked, but I'm not sure what I'm doing.

"For a few nights," I tell her as I sit down while focusing on the cookies. "They smell lovely," I say, and she bustles over to the coffee machine first, where she fills me a mug. I sit at the breakfast bar and watch her move around the kitchen.

Mary moves fast, but she's a stout woman with short curly hair that's always wild. Her hair is kind of like mine: unmanageable.

A tray with milk, coffee, sugar, and cookies is placed in front of me as Liam comes into the kitchen. The atmosphere instantly changes. Mary doesn't like him, and she doesn't hide it. Liam, to me, has always been different. But he doesn't scare me off.

"Cookie?" I offer him. His eyes flicker to the cookie, and he actually takes it. Not what I was expecting. Nor do I expect it when he sits down across from me.

He could be a model, waiting to have a photo taken. He isn't exactly fully sitting on the stool; one foot rests on the floor. He unbuttons his suit jacket and rests one hand on his leg. He has no idea how he appears as he eats the cookie. I want to laugh, but I don't. Instead, I pour my coffee and thank Mary as she leaves the room.

"How are you, Una?" He doesn't glance up at me as he speaks, his focus solely on the cookie that he still eats. His words are filled with boredom, like somehow, he's being forced to make small talk.

"Great, and you Liam?" I ask. Some amusement has slipped into my words, and he peers up at me.

"I have no complaints at all, Una." His monotone voice has me hiding a smile behind my coffee mug. He gets up and bids me a good day. Nothing weird or odd about that at all.

I spend the next hour searching the house and grounds for Shane with no luck. I find Darragh and Finn fighting in Darragh's room. My mind takes in the floor, which is covered in clothes. Darragh's room is like a teenager's, and he has banned Mary from cleaning it.

"Okay, okay. Calm down." I step in between them. It hasn't come to blows, but it doesn't seem like that's far off.

"Una, this is private." Finn's sharp words sting, but I fold my arms across my chest.

"And what? Let you kill each other?" I ask.

"Don't fucking speak to her like that," Darragh jumps to my defense, and I snap my gaze to him. His jaw is red, and his fists are clenched. I'm not sure what has him wound up, but seeing Darragh angry is odd.

"It's a private conversation. That's all I said," Finn replies. He's calmer now.

"It's my fucking room. And Una stays."

"You know what…" Finn doesn't finish his sentence but storms out of the room. I watch him leave, silently questioning what has everyone fired up. I turn to Darragh to ask, but he throws himself on his unmade bed.

"Don't ask," he says, and his serious tone has me leaving it alone.

"Your room is disgusting," I tell him, glancing around me. How does he live like this?

"Yeah, it is," he agrees and starts to smile. "Want to go to a party?"

The "party" that Darragh takes me to is in a small village. The pub has locked its doors, so we're free to party. Smoking is prohibited in all pubs, but here, I walk through another cloud of smoke. The smoking isn't the worst that's happening here. Most people are high and jump around as a guy with a red long beard beats the shit out of a bodhrán.

Darragh takes my hand and pulls me through the crowd. He looks alive as he smiles at me, and I find myself loosening up.

"Una, this is Brian." I'm introduced to a really good-looking guy. He's tall, with wavy blond hair and sparkling blue eyes I could fall into.

He gives me a quick glance, but his attention is back on Darragh. "You better have brought my money."

I focus on the floor as Darragh smiles and promises his way out of not having the money for Brian. I steal glances at Brian. He knows he's attractive.

All eyes are on me, and it's for the wrong reasons. I wish I had tied my hair up and put on some sunglasses. But the more rebellious side of me sticks out my tongue at them. It's fun, and when Darragh swings around and places a pink pill on my outstretched tongue, I swallow it with a long drink from the bottle that I hold.

Time moves in a funny pattern. I'm dancing. All the colors—I can't catch them. The vehicle under us is moving. Blond hair and blue eyes fill my vision.

"Brian," I manage to say, and everyone laughs. I'm sitting in the pool house. Brian's there again, and his lips move against mine, his tongue forcing its way into my mouth. The weight of a small tablet registers with me as he passes it into my mouth, and I swallow.

The tiles under my feet are cold but shiny. They move like water. I touch them, and they bark at me.

"Una, leave the dog alone," someone shouts. The beast moves toward me, and I run toward the light. I know its safety. I'm in a glass house. Water fills my mouth, and I can't breathe. Someone pulls me back.

A girl laughs. "What are you doing in the shower?"

Shower. A solid cold pane of glass presses against my fingers. I'm in the shower. She puts something into her mouth while offering me a small pink pill. I decline. I'm aware that what's happening is happening, but it seems like it isn't.

She shrugs and puts the second pill in her mouth. I watch her slide slowly to the ground. I reach out to her, but my head collides with glass, and I find myself on the ground with her.

Laughter bubbles from my mouth. Large legs cross my vision. I see blond hair from the back. "Brian," I whisper, and he grins down at me. He's so tall; he's like one hundred feet high.

I try to reach out to him, but my hand is tiny. "My hand!" I panic, but he laughs, and I laugh too. Brian's mouth is huge, stretching and growing, and I blink a few times before the darkness consumes me. I try to fight it, but it's no good.

CHAPTER FOUR

O'REAGAN
AN CHLANN

UNA

Three people lie beside me, their hands behind their heads. I blink and three becomes one. My stomach tightens with the pain that rips through it. I manage to crawl to the shower, where I heave. Every glance I flicker toward the girl on the floor doesn't make her move. I want her to move; my brain is telling me she's too still, too pale. My hands tremble as I wipe wet hair from my forehead. I notice then that I'm soaking wet.

I'm looking around the bathroom, trying to make sense of this. I need someone to tell me what happened. I use the tiles to hoist myself up; standing is a challenge I somehow manage. I'm so cold. *How long have I been lying here?* My attention draws to the girl again. From this angle, I can see her face fully, and she's dead.

Her coloring isn't natural, nor is the stillness of her chest. I've never done CPR, but I know I can't stand here and do nothing. My hand trembles as I reach out to her while kneeling down, covering one hand with my other one as I close my eyes.

You can do this, Una.

Slowly, I open my eyes. I try again, but I can't touch her. She's dead. I know she's dead. I move back away from the body and glance around the room. Once again, no one is here. The floor is rising and falling as I rock back and forth. A single black marble tile becomes my sole focus as I try to calm myself, but it isn't working.

It's wet, and I reach out and touch it. The tips of my fingers turn red. I yank my hand back to my chest. My breaths are bursting from my lungs, and I can't stop blinking as I stare at the body.

"What happened?" Arms pull at me. The dead girl disappears, and Darragh's face fills my vision.

"She's dead." My words are a whisper.

"What happened to you? Da is going to kill me." A burning pain ignites in my head as Darragh's fingers brush across my forehead. Automatically, my own hand joins his. My fingers are red when I glance at them.

Darragh moves out of my line of vision, and the dead girl is back.

"She's dead," I whimper, and this time, Darragh seems to hear me. He's returned with a towel, but he doesn't put it to my head. Instead, he joins me in staring at the dead girl.

"She's dead?" he questions.

"Yes." I can't process this. *What will happen to me? Will I go to prison? Was it me who killed her? Was it the drugs? Who will be held responsible? Okay, Michael is going to kill us for bringing this into his home. My mother?* My mind is growing more frantic.

"She's dead." Darragh's shout snaps me out of my own inner turmoil. He paces the floor. A vein bulges in his neck as he roars. "Fuck. We are so fucked."

Tears burn my eyes at his words. "Do something," I tell him as I start to rock again.

"This isn't my mess." His calm accusation knocks me out of my state.

"Darragh, this is your party. There is a dead girl in your bathroom." Now I'm the one shouting.

"Everything okay?" someone asks through the door.

Darragh stares at the door, and I stare at him. We can't let anyone else see this. I get up and make sure the door is locked.

"Yeah, be out in a minute," I say and wait for a few seconds. Darragh is fixated on the body.

"Darragh, give me your phone." I don't have a clue where mine is, so I hold out my hand.

"What do you want my phone for?" Confusion fills his voice. It must be the shock.

"To ring the Gardaí and an ambulance. We need to report this."

He turns his back on me, shaking his head.

"Darragh, we need to report this." I shiver again at the thoughts of what will happen to me. But leaving her lying on a cold tile floor seems wrong.

"Darragh," I shout and get his attention.

"Yeah, I'll ring. You get rid of everyone." He seems together, and I find myself nodding. He comes to me, and I want to roar, crying in his arms, but he moves my hair.

"We need to cover the cut so no one asks questions," he says before stepping away. His coldness is something I've never seen before, but I tell myself it's the shock. A dead body isn't something either of us has seen before.

There are three people left in the pool house, and they are easy to shift. No one seems to search for the dead girl, and I feel relief and guilt that no one remembers her. I search the room for a bag or jacket—something to give the guards so they can identify her— but there's nothing in the room. When I return to the bathroom, I find Darragh sitting beside her, having a fag.

"How long will they be?" I ask, and he gapes at me with that confused stare again. "You go on to bed. I'll sort this."

I laugh. "Go to bed?" My chest is tight, and I'm struggling to breathe. I don't need him to go into shock on me. I need him to be strong until the Gardaí get here.

"Fuck's sake, Una." He's up quicker than I expect. Throwing the half-smoked cigarette into the sink, he marches toward me and yanks me by the arm.

"What are you doing?" I ask, trying to get free, but Darragh is stronger than he looks.

"Go to bed," he says before leading me out of the pool house. I'm left standing outside, freezing and confused. Darragh glances back at me over his shoulder. He looks focused and angry, but he doesn't appear to be in any kind of shock.

SHANE

I check my phone. It's four in the morning. I'm not sure what woke me. I lie back down as I hear another loud noise coming from down the hall. I climb out of bed, pull on jeans, and grab the bat from behind my door.

The hall is dark, and I keep it that way while moving along the wall slowly. My bare feet help keep me soundless. I start to realize it isn't an intruder as light shines under the door from the fourth bedroom down from mine. Also, an intruder wouldn't be as noisy. Another bang sounds before a female voice curses.

What is Una doing? I lower the bat but still keep it in my hands as I open the door. She's wet again. This girl has a thing for water. She's searching for something in the wardrobe. In the process, she's knocking boxes and clothes onto the ground.

"What are you doing?" I ask.

She spins around, her wet long hair flicking water with the speed of her movements. The wildness in her eyes has my stomach tightening. I'm beside her, searching her face. Her gaze lowers, and she shakes her head.

"Una, what's wrong?" I ask the crown of her head, and

when she peeks up at me, her eyes are watery. She stares at me, unblinking. A tremble has entered her body, and my heart starts to pound.

"Una, what's wrong?" I ask again. I want to grab her and shake her, but touching her has never been a luxury I've allowed myself. Right now, I seem unable to move.

"I can't find dry clothes." She blinks and tears fall. I loosen my grip on the bat.

"Because this isn't your room," I tell her, taking a step out of the wardrobe, but she doesn't follow.

She moves around the wardrobe like it's her first time seeing it. She's shaking as she slowly skims her fingers across a pile of blankets. There's blood on her hands. I take her wrist as I step back into the wardrobe, and she flinches at the contact as her eyes widen. I've dealt with blood before, but her blood is doing something entirely different to me.

I'm searching her face, her arms, but I can't see anything.

"It's my head. I don't… I don't know…"

I find it quickly. It's a deep gash. "We need to get you to the hospital."

She's shaking her head. "I didn't know."

I don't have a clue what she's babbling about. Her standing here, bleeding and cold, isn't doing any good for my heart. "It's fine. Let's get you sorted first." I smile when she nods. Finally, I can take care of her.

When I release her wrist, her eyes widen, and she shakes her head again. "We need to go to the pool house." She moves past me, and I'm trying to catch up with her.

"Una, why?" I'm whisper-shouting, not wanting to wake up anyone else.

"Shit." It's not until I'm out in the courtyard that I remember I have no shoes and no shirt on. The cold air has me moving faster after Una. All I want to do is get her head looked at and out of those wet clothes.

The pool house is a mess, the embers of a party dying slowly.

"Una." I call her again as she makes her way to the bathroom. Her blue lips and pale skin have me itching to get her to a doctor, and whatever she wants to show me, I'll check out so we can go. I curse Darragh because I know this is his doing. He's a heavy hitter when it comes to partying, and I question now if Una is on something. I'm going to kill him.

Una steps inside the bathroom, and I follow her. What I find isn't what I was expecting. Darragh is sitting beside a girl—a girl whose lips are blue. Her body lies limply on the floor.

Darragh's eyes snap up to mine as I step into the bathroom. I try to control my anger as I take in the mess before me.

"She's dead." Una's crying beside me, but all I take in is Darragh. What a screwup.

"Get the fuck up," I tell him, and he jumps up quickly. I check the girl for a pulse and don't find one at first, but there's a flicker of life there.

"What has she taken?" I ask Darragh, and he shrugs.

"You are so fucking useless." He lowers his head. Una is still shaking, her eyes shooting everywhere. She's in shock.

"Una. I need you to focus, sweetheart." Her eyes snap to me, and she blinks, allowing more tears to fall. "She isn't dead. But what has she taken?"

She moves quickly to get beside me. Her bare arm brushes mine, and I hold my breath at the contact.

"She isn't?" She's smiling, her fingers moving up my arm, and I'm staring into her eyes, not sure how to sort through everything. I need her to stop touching me. Her eyes search the floor as if she can see the past play out before her. "She took pills." Her head snaps up, and she's almost excited with this information.

Darragh takes out a pack of fags, getting ready to light one up. "Darragh, take Una back to the house and get her dry clothes. Then take her to my car where I will meet you. We need to get both girls to the hospital. You think you can manage that?"

"Yeah, yeah, of course," he answers like a fucking victim. He makes me sick. Turning to Una as she clings to my arm, I force a smile.

"Go with Darragh. Everything will be okay."

She's nodding, but it's like she's boneless. The adrenaline is leaving her body. I snap my head to Darragh, and he helps Una stand.

I wait until they've left the room before I hoist the girl off the ground. I'm trying to wake her, but shaking her and even slapping her across the face doesn't have any impact. She's getting cold. *Did I imagine the flicker of a heartbeat?* I check again, and it's still there.

I bend her over before opening her mouth and sticking my fingers down her throat. Nothing happens at first, but she starts gagging before sick pours over my hand and out onto the floor. I hold her up as liquid continues to pour from her. I repeat the action until there's nothing left for her to bring up.

When she pushes my arms away, I lift her up onto the counter and get her a glass of water; she brings back up the first sip but manages to keep the second mouthful down.

I leave the girl there as I return to the house and get dressed.

She's still in the same place when I return. I carry her to the garage. Una sits in the front of the car. Her eyes are wide, and I can see the quick rise and fall of her chest as she stares at the girl. She's in dry clothes, and that relaxes me until my gaze settles on Darragh sitting in the back of my car. I open the door.

"Get out," I tell him, and he does as I place the girl in the back. Once I have the door closed, I turn to Darragh and grab him by the neck.

"You're such a fucking waste. Go tell Liam the mess you made while I take these two to the hospital." I let him go, pushing him away from me, and he rubs his neck. His anger, I can see, and

I almost want him to put his hands on me so I can hurt him. But he turns away and goes back into the house.

Una wrings her hands as I start to drive to Navan. It's the closest hospital to us.

"How's your head?" I ask, and she shoots me a sideways glance. She pulls her lip between her teeth and chews on it.

I need to focus on the road and not Una.

"It's sore now. I didn't really notice it earlier."

I nod. "It was the adrenaline that was keeping it at bay. We're nearly there, so you'll be seen soon." She isn't sitting as straight anymore. "Una, don't fall asleep." I flicker a glance at her, and she rubs her eyes.

"I'm so sleepy all of a sudden." Her words are slurred.

"Yeah, it's the cut on your head. You've lost a lot of blood. It's important that you don't sleep, okay?"

"Okay." I don't like her one-word response.

"Stephen told me you saw the horse I got you," I say, and straight away, I regret it. It's not her reaction—she sits a bit straighter—but it's how it makes me feel. It was the first time I tried to show her I cared.

She had been so excited that day, and getting her the horse was the best decision I had ever made. But as she had sat proudly on top of the horse, Dad had squeezed my shoulder. His words had my stomach tightening. "You're a good brother to her."

The way I looked at her wasn't how a brother looked at a sister. I had shrugged his arm off. "She's not my sister." My angry words were heard by all, even Una, as I stormed off.

"Yeah, she's the best." Her words are still slurred, but she's happy and she's talking. "I'm not sure if I ever thanked you." She reaches for my arm, but her hand flops down halfway across. I glance at her, and she's smiling at me with lids half-closed.

"You're welcome, Una," I tell her before focusing on the road. I remember the day I saw the horse. She was wild. The handler wasn't able to control her, and all I saw was Una. I knew they would be a perfect match, and I was right. "We're nearly there."

She shifts, pulling herself up more. The sign for Navan has me lifting my foot off the pedal, but I still move quickly through the empty town. It takes five more minutes before I pull up outside the Emergency Room. Department.

I open Una's door and help her out. The fresh air has her eyes opening a bit wider. I close the door and lock the car, leaving the other girl in the back. She's asleep, and my number one priority is Una. For now, she seems to have forgotten about the girl. She allows me to lead her into ER, where a few people wait. I smile at the receptionist. She doesn't return the smile as I give Una's details.

"Fill out this form and take a seat." She slides the form to me.

"I'd like to be seen now," I tell her, glaring over her shoulder in search of a doctor.

"And so would the man behind you with only three fingers. We're moving as fast as we can." I don't look at the man in question. This place makes my skin crawl. I hate being so close to other sick people. I direct Una to a seat and kneel down in front of her.

"I'm going to step out for a moment, but I'll be back," I tell her.

She's far more alert. Her eyes focus on my face, and my stomach tightens. My thumb brushes her thigh, and she jerks. I quickly get up and go outside.

I carry in the girl, and the receptionist raises an eyebrow. I give her another smile, and yet again, she doesn't return it. "I found her on the sidewalk. I think she's taken something," I tell the receptionist.

"Her name?" she asks with fingers hovering over the keyboard.

The girl is heavy, and I move her to the closest seat and sit her up, but she slumps over. The receptionist continues to observe me.

"I don't know," I answer and return to Una. I've done my part. Now I need to figure out what the hell we're going to do with Darragh.

Vicious

CHAPTER FIVE

O'REAGAN
AN CHLANN

UNA

My head hurts. I get four stitches and strict orders to stay awake for the next twelve hours as a precaution. I'm waiting to be discharged, and Shane is sitting in a plastic chair while he scrolls through his phone. I still can't believe all he's done for me tonight. When he peers up at me, my pulse spikes. I want to ask him why he's being kind to me, but the doctor returns.

"Okay. You're all set to go." He hands me a prescription. "If the pain persists, take one every four hours." I'm nodding as Shane rises and tucks his phone into his pocket.

He reaches out his hand to the doctor. "Thank you," he tells him, and the doctor takes his hand. The silver band on his thumb reflects the light, grabbing my attention. My eyes roam up his arm, where a small band of black is visible, but it quickly disappears under the sleeve of his jumper. When my eyes meet his, my heart leaps in my chest.

"Ready to go?" he asks, and I give a quick smile and get down off the bed. "I'll take that." Shane reaches out his hand for the prescription, and I give it to him.

He's always careful not to touch me. But earlier, I could have sworn his thumb stroked my thigh. Maybe I imagined it. My head wasn't exactly in a good place.

Back in the car is the first time my mind wanders to the girl. "The girl, is she okay?"

Shane starts the car and pulls out of the hospital parking lot. The sun is up. It's nine in the morning, and I'm sleepy, exhausted from everything.

"Yeah. They pumped her stomach, but she's going to be fine." Shane focuses on the road as he drives, and I steal glances at him. This is the longest I've ever been in his company, and my opinion of him has changed. I always fancied him but never got close to him. He wasn't an easy person to get close to.

We don't go home. Instead, Shane pulls up at Whitewood Lake. There's a fog sitting on the water. I don't move as Shane climbs out of the car and walks around to my side. I unbuckle my seat belt as he opens the door.

"I thought the fresh air might help keep you awake." I step out of the car, and he places a large jacket around my shoulders.

Now all I smell is Shane, his cologne along with the scent of leather and trees. It's a weird combination, but it's uniquely Shane. My stomach trembles as he leans around me and closes the door.

Shane walks with his hands behind his back, but there's a bounce in his step. He doesn't seem like someone who has been up half the night. I can only imagine my appearance, but instead of focusing on that, I give all my attention to Shane.

"Do you know that Whitewood Lake has its very own monster?" I love the lilt that enters Shane's words. It makes me glance at him, and I see his small grin. I find myself smiling at him.

"I've been around these parts for a long time, and I've never heard anything about a monster," I say. His grin expands into a smile, and my heart skips a beat. But I don't lose eye contact. His beauty entrances me.

"In 1981, it was spotted and sounded similar to the Loch Ness monster."

"May be a relative," I answer, and Shane gives a small laugh that has my stomach erupting in butterflies.

We're silent for a moment, and I find myself staring into the water, questioning if things like monsters really are under the murky surface. Shane walks on the inside; he's closer to the rippling waves. He seems at peace, his face relaxed and a constant smile visible. My mind goes back to what happened, and most of all, Darragh.

"Can I ask you something?" We stop near two large trees, and I'm nervous now that Shane is facing me. His brown eyes are like orbs of chocolate; they could really pull a girl in. I'm so sleep-deprived that I can't focus for a second.

"Of course." Shane folds his arms across his broad chest as he stares out at the water. A chest I saw bare a few hours ago. To see him standing in only a pair of jeans in the closet had nearly undone me. He's waiting patiently, and I pull my mind from the gutter.

"When I thought the girl was dead, Darragh was supposed to ring the Gardaí, but he didn't." I chew my bottom lip, pondering if I had said the right thing. Shane is his brother, after all, and I don't know what I'm even trying to say.

"Maybe he was in shock," Shane tells the lake.

"Yeah, maybe," I respond, but I don't believe it. I don't know what I believe, but he wasn't in shock. It doesn't really matter, I suppose, since it turned out all right. I pull Shane's jacket tighter around me, trying to smell it without making it noticeable. Shane takes my movements for me being cold, and he shoos me back to the car.

I don't argue and I don't remove the jacket, but Shane

doesn't ask for it. His phone rings, and he struggles to get it out of his pocket.

"Need a hand?" I ask, and his no is resounding and quick. I sit back, a sting of embarrassment snapping my head away. He manages to get the phone out and answers it. I want to tell him that driving and talking on a phone is illegal, but I do it all the time.

It's Liam on the other end of the phone. "I can't talk," Shane says. "Yeah, we'll talk when I get home." There's more of Liam's voice, but I can't understand what's being said. But Shane laughs, and it's not a sweet laugh. "Like I said, we'll talk later." He hangs up without saying goodbye, and the car moves faster under us.

"Everything okay?" I ask after a moment, and he slows down slightly.

"Yeah. Just Liam being Liam." We pull into the drive, and I feel disappointed that my time with Shane will end. I don't speak as we make our way up the drive.

I expect Shane to pull into the garage, but he doesn't. Instead, he drives out back and through the courtyard, and we pull up outside the stables. I glance at him, but his fingers drum on the steering wheel as he faces forward. He doesn't speak as he climbs out, and once again, he opens my door for me.

"I thought you might like to check in on your horse." He's holding open my door, but he isn't looking at me, and now I question what Liam said to him. He seems far away. As I get out, he's still holding the door, my face flush with his chest.

"Shane," I whisper, and my stomach twists as he looks down at me. My heart starts to pound as he stares at me.

"Good morning, Mr. O'Reagan." Shane gapes at Stephen like he materialized from thin air. Shane steps out of my way and gives me a quick nod. He greets Stephen stiffly. This is the Shane I've become accustomed to, the one who treats the staff like tools and not people.

"Morning, Stephen. How is she today?" I ask as I make my way down to the stables. Stephen walks beside me.

"She's a lot better. Still can't touch her, but I'm confident you can." He's grinning at me as he veers off to do his jobs. I stop at my horse's stable, and Shane stands a few feet away. He doesn't join me. I'm not sure what he's doing, but I open the door and step into the stall. She moves back as I slowly approach but settles as I place my hand on her before leaning into her coat. My face heats up against her skin.

"She was kicking and bucking the day I saw her. She was uncontrollable, and the handlers couldn't break her."

I lean out as Shane steps into the stable with his hands behind his back. He doesn't make any attempt to rub her or come closer as he tells me about the horse.

"She had reared back, and her mane caught the sun, and I don't know…" He frowns. "I thought of you."

My heart flutters at his words.

"She was unpredictable." He looks at me for the first time. "Untamable."

My pulse spikes with how he looks at me, and it might be the lack of sleep, but I feel like I've stepped into a twilight zone with Shane. It's like that feeling when you're lying under the stars knowing the world is asleep. It's magical, but it has to end.

"I remember that day also Shane. When you told everyone how I wasn't your sister." It was childish of me, but it had hurt. He said it with such disgust that it's stayed with me through the years. I never looked at him as a brother, but it was the disgust in his voice that had shattered me. I remember thinking that I couldn't blame him with how odd I was, and odd isn't always good.

The moment I flicker my gaze at Shane, I regret my words. His jaw is clenched, his shoulders tense. At least I know he remembers. I didn't really expect that.

"Sorry, that was childish," I say quickly. "It was a long time ago."

He shakes his head. "No, I hurt you."

My throat burns as he speaks, because he really had hurt me.

"It's fine," I say as I continue to run my hands along my horse. When Shane's hand rubs close to mine, I freeze along with the animal under us.

"I'm sorry." His words are low and precise, like he's trying out a new language. I glance at him, causing our shoulders to brush, and this time, it looks like he's the one who freezes. He takes a step away from the horse and me. "You need to eat." The declaration is like a light bulb going off over his head, and I can't help the smile that grows on my face.

"I do?" I question, and he smiles, sending butterflies scattering to the corners of my stomach.

"Yes, you do," he says before leaving.

I shake my head while I give my horse a final rub. I glance around me, making sure that Shane is gone and Stephen can't see me before I bury my face in Shane's coat and inhale.

A giggle erupts from me. I'm acting crazy. It was the bang to the head that's causing me to act odd, I decide as I lock the stables and make my way to the house.

The kitchen is warm, and Mary smiles at me the moment I enter. "Una, I'm making your favorite."

The smell of pancakes has me drooling. I didn't expect to see Shane sitting at the table. It's set for two people. He's on his phone, fingers moving rapidly across the screen. He has such a serious expression on his face.

"Orders from Master Shane," Mary adds and that grabs my attention and Shane's.

"Master Shane?" I question, not wanting to mention the fact that he knows pancakes are my favorite.

"Sit down, Una." The demand is sharp and comes from Shane.

I don't like it. I shed his jacket and place it on the chair, but I don't sit. He flashes a glance toward Mary as she prepares pancakes and coffee before they snap back to me.

"Please." He says it through gritted teeth, but I take it and sit down. I'm sitting across from him, and the setting is almost intimate except for the bustle of Mary. Shane focuses on his phone, and I take in the circles under his eyes.

"You should go to bed," I tell him.

"I'm fine." He doesn't glance up from his phone as he answers me. Mary places a coffee in front of me, but she pauses as she hovers over me. "What happened to your head, sweetheart?" I had almost forgotten about it.

"Oh—" I start to explain, but Shane cuts me off.

He stands up and takes the paper from his pocket before handing it to Mary. It's my prescription. "I'll finish up here. You go and get the prescription."

Mary glances at me and hesitates, and it's like I can see the wheels turning in her head as she looks from me to Shane. The way she glances from me to Shane makes it appear like she thinks Shane did this to my head.

"I fell," I tell her. As she moves back slightly, her eyes widen, then they narrow in disbelief.

"Why are you still here?" Shane's words are quiet, but they would move a stone. She leaves quickly, and Shane is up, making pancakes. I've lost my appetite.

This is how I remember him with the staff—an actual asshole. I don't speak even as he puts a plate of steaming pancakes in front of me. They aren't as perfectly circular as I've become used to, but he buttered and sugared them just as I like. A jug of maple syrup is on the table, and I don't hold back in coating them in the sticky substance.

"I really shouldn't eat your pancakes since you were so rude to Mary," I say as Shane sits down.

He's rolled up his sleeves, his tattoo on display. It's an odd one; large, thick black bands circle his arm. I often wondered what it meant but never asked. "No, you should starve yourself. That way, I'll be kinder to Mary."

He takes a forkful of the pancakes, and I'm transfixed on his mouth as he chews. He doesn't show any remorse as he pauses and raises an eyebrow.

"Eat, Una," he tells me once his mouth is empty, and I gaze at him as he refills his mouth.

Before I lose all self-control, I start to eat the best pancakes in the world. "Okay, these are delicious," I tell him. Shane has finished his, and he watches me eat mine. I can't stop smiling in between mouthfuls. "Why are you watching me?" I ask, but I don't mind that he is.

"Why are you smiling?" he fires back.

"Because you're watching me."

He smiles, and I shake my head. He's gorgeous. "I've been thinking about your job."

I don't like the change in topic, but I try to hold the smile. I want to talk about why he's watching me, eat not some stupid job. I sugar and milk my coffee. "Let's hear it," I say, and he sits back.

"I need a bookkeeper." He waves his hand in my direction, like he made me, the bookkeeper, appear.

I'm shaking my head, and he sits back, his recent confidence leaving. "What you've done for me tonight is more than anyone ever has," I answer honestly. When he leans in, his eyes crinkle at the corners, but I hold my hand up, knowing I need to finish.

"Seriously, I can't thank you enough. But working with numbers... I can't." I clean a spot on the table that isn't dirty. I swallow, surprised by the level of emotion that's coming with my words. "I'm not her. I don't want to be her. I'm not my mother, Shane."

His eyes light up with understanding. "You don't want to be an accountant?" he asks, and I nod my head, trying to keep the tears back. "So what do you want to do?" Shane takes a drink of his own coffee, and his brown eyes have softened.

"That's it? You're not going to try to convince me that I'm throwing my whole future away?" I'm not sure if that's what I want to hear, but it's what I'm used to hearing. So having someone accept what I'm saying is a shock.

"When dad asked me to get you a job, I don't recall him telling me to make you miserable." His small smile has my heart beating faster.

"I know what I want to do." My heart is racing. The idea that I could do what I truly love is rushing the blood through my body. "I want to work with Stephen. Help out with the horses." It was Shane buying me the horse that made my love for horses grow.

It's because of him, in a way, that I no longer want to be an accountant. That I want to be free. Be me. I should be thanking him for more than tonight.

"Okay, we can organize that."

I'm beaming with joy. "Seriously?" I ask, and Shane's eyes are soft as he smiles at me. It sends butterflies erupting in my stomach.

"Yes. It's so nice to see you happy."

I'm a little speechless right now. I'm ready to burst with so many emotions as I take a drink of coffee. Glancing at Shane over my cup, my pulse spikes as our eyes clash.

"Thank you." It's nearly a whisper, but it's the most heartfelt thank you I've ever given.

"You're welcome," Shane says with a slight nod. We sit and sip coffee while staring at each other. It's perfect until Liam walks in, and I know our time together is up.

CHAPTER SIX

O'REAGAN
AN CHLANN

SHANE

There's the smallest smudge of blood near her hairline; I notice it when she tilts her head. Otherwise, her face is flawless. Her skin has a shine to it. It's like the beauty inside her is trying to shine through. I love watching her mouth when she smiles. It's as fascinating as her different-colored eyes.

I take another sip of coffee and continue to take her in. She's sleepy, her lids dropping every few seconds, but we both sit up as Liam enters the kitchen. He's rang a few times, and we need to talk.

"How are you feeling, Una?" His words are precise as he speaks to her, and I want him to stop. I'm not entirely sure why. Maybe because he makes her uncomfortable. Maybe because he normally doesn't interact, so why with Una?

"I've had the best nurse take care of me," she tells him as she smiles at me, but there's a sadness in her eyes that I don't understand.

"I see. We need to speak." His attention is on me, and that sits better on my shoulders. I get up and ring Finn.

"Una's in the kitchen. I can't stay with her, so I need you to watch over her for the next few hours." Una tries to object, but I keep my back to her. Finn agrees. I don't glance back at Una as I follow Liam out the door.

We go to my bedroom. I'm exhausted, and this day hasn't ended yet. I sit on my bed and start pulling off my top. Liam stands along the wall. He never sits. He never appears comfortable.

Now I question what my brother's relationships with women must be like. I've never really thought about it before—I never cared—but spending the day with Una makes me question if he's ever felt like that. I put on a clean T-shirt and sit back down on my bed.

"Did you talk to Darragh?" I ask, pulling off my boots and socks.

"Yes, and Darragh is the least of your worries." Liam's controlled words make me want to lose control. I snort.

"Darragh is a huge problem, Liam. You'll have to see it sooner rather than later. He's going to get one of us killed. One of us," I state, pointing at myself.

"You can't punish him for something that hasn't happened."

I grit my teeth. "You can't ignore the signs that something *will* happen, Liam. Give him time."

"I'll have a word with Finn."

I'm shaking my head even as Liam says it. Finn has always been Darragh's babysitter, but he isn't going to solve this. Finn hasn't been himself since Connor disappeared. To me, the solution to this is to find Connor.

"A new supplier has moved into the area. He's trying to take over three of our areas. Dad wants it stopped and cleaned up straight away."

I rest my elbows on my knees. This isn't good. "A name?" I ask, but Liam is already shaking his head.

"Nothing. But Dad's informant said Dublin will be the first hit."

I snort again while glaring up at the ceiling. "Dad's famous informant. I don't suppose he told you who it was?" I ask, already knowing the answer. But Liam is moving to the door; this conversation is over.

"You need to sleep." I don't wait until he's gone before I climb into bed. I dream of Whitewood Lake and monsters.

I wake up and immediately check my phone. It's six in the evening. I've slept for roughly four or five hours. I can't even remember what time I went to bed. My mind is still circling back to the monster in the lake with a mix of my conversation with Liam.

I'm out of bed, making my way down the hall, and once I push open the door, something twists in my stomach as I take in all her curly red hair fanned out around her head like a burning halo.

Her cheeks are pink, and I can relax at the rise and fall of her chest. She's wearing a white top, the straps only strings, allowing me to see a lot of milky skin. I should wake her and make sure she's okay. A concussion was a very high risk with someone in her case. I gently and carefully shake her arm that's covered by the blanket.

"Una," I say gently as I shake her, but she doesn't stir. While standing back, I stare at her. Nothing. I try again, shaking her with more force.

"Una, wake up." It's a little too loud, and she sits up quickly, nearly colliding into me, but I'm quick and jump back. I don't get the smiling girl I had in the kitchen. Una's eyes are narrowed as she glares at me, her chest rising and falling quickly.

"What is with this family? You guys like waking me up."

"Who else wakes you up?" I fire back dryly, not liking that idea at all.

She shakes her head. "What do you want, Shane?" She's almost barking, and I drop the whole subject of someone waking her up. But I will ask her another time, when she's not ready to kill me.

"Go back to sleep, Una," I tell her, and her eyes grow in size. I want to smile. She's beautiful in the morning, but I know better.

"Go back to sleep, Una! Well, what did you wake me up for?" She's shouting, and I can't help but smile as I make my way to the door

"To make sure you were alive," I say as a shoe hits the wall an inch from me.

"Can a dead person throw shoes?" She's red in the cheeks with temper.

"They say redheads have foul tempers. Now I have proof that it's true." I make it out the door in one piece as something else hits the wall. I assume the other shoe.

I shower and change before getting into my car and making my way to a meeting in Dublin with one of our main customers.

It takes me forty minutes to reach The Marker hotel, where I set up the meeting. I park in the underground parking before making my way up to the veranda. As the doors open, I'm greeted by a member of the staff. "Mr. O' Reagan."

I nod in greeting as I'm taken outside to my seat. Overhead heaters keep the area warm, but the night's not cold. The large couch is comfortable, and I sit down, peering out over the city. Lights sparkle from the hundreds of windows, and it makes me think that Una would like it here. I've never appreciated the view, but I would love to see it from her eyes.

"The usual, Mr. O'Reagan? Should I bring it now or wait for your guest to arrive?" The waiter stands next to the table, one hand behind his back.

"You can bring it now and double the usual," I tell him, and he leaves as Gary arrives. Gary is a bull in a suit. That's what comes to mind when I take in his huge frame. The gray suit he wears could tear at the wrong movement. The white collar is open; he couldn't close it even if he wanted to. His neck is as thick as three men's.

He takes off his sunglasses as he sits down and puts them on the table. It's dark outside, so the sunglasses aren't necessary.

"Got to say, I was surprised when I heard you wanted to meet me. I'm not in trouble, am I?" Gary smiles. Meeting me isn't necessary very often, unless prices go up or we've run into a problem.

The waiter arrives back and places a brandy in front of us. "You're not in trouble. Relax," I reply to Gary, and he rubs his hands together while sitting back with his drink.

Gary reminded me of a Ken doll, but no matter his appearance, he wasn't stupid. He didn't supply nearly all of Dublin with drugs by being stupid.

"I wanted to check on business," I say and take a drink, relaxing back into the orange couch. Gary hasn't the same level of comfort that I have. The wicker chair is larger than most, but it wouldn't have the same space or comfort as the couch.

"Yeah, it's good." His eyes slightly narrow. "It's about the new supplier."

I clap for a moment. "Right to it. I like that, Gary. So what can you tell me?" I take a drink. He shifts in his seat before leaning forward. The joking Gary is gone now, and I'm eye to eye with the businessman.

"Look, his product is clean. I don't know where he's making it or how. But it's cheap, and it's huge in London."

"What's his name?" I ask, and Gary leans back, opening his arms.

"Come on, Shane. You know I can't do that. You're not losing me as a customer. It's just that this guy has a new product."

A product I'm sure we could replicate. "Do you have a sample?"

"On me? No man. Gardaí everywhere."

I don't fully believe Gary. I don't trust any of my customers. A man who can take a life isn't an easy man to figure out, and Gary has taken a lot of lives.

"I need a name, Gary."

He tilts his head at my request, as if to say he doesn't know.

"Have you ever met my brother, Liam?" I ask, and he sits back again.

"Bernard," he finally coughs up.

"I didn't do anything." Neill has his hands in the air. He's four foot nothing, an easy target, but I'm not here to hurt him. After leaving Gary, I decided to drop in on an old 'family' friend.

"Is that how you answer your door?" I ask, and he quickly drops his arms and lets me in. I double-check that my Audi is locked. It's a council estate, and black wood from a recent burning still sits in the center of the play area outside Neill's house.

The sitting room holds battered couches. Neill scoots around me and turns off the television, but I catch what he was watching. When I return my gaze to him, he shrugs.

"I might be small in height, but I'm big in other ways," he tells me as he sits down on the couch.

I'm not here to talk about his dick, so I don't. I sit down in the armchair across from him. "Any new fighters or people moving through your circle recently?" I ask. Connor was his number one fighter, and he made a lot of money off my brother.

His feet dangle. They don't reach the floor as he sits back in the couch. His white tracksuit is cheap and a copy of a popular brand.

"A few new ones. None like Connor." He's smiling with genuine affection for Connor. Connor isn't exactly the friendly type. I often see him as a mix of us all. At times, he reminds me of Liam, but he can be a mess like Darragh—only, Darragh is women and drugs, where Connor is fighting and drink.

"Have you heard the name Bernard going around?" The moment I ask, I can see he's heard of him. His eyebrows lift at the same time.

"Yeah, I have. He's been supplying some new drug. Some of his men were giving out samples at one of my fights, but I ran them off."

"You personally?" I know he didn't, but I can't let this conversation go by without him understanding that I could crush him.

"No, my bouncers. Shane, I respect you and your family. You have my word that I'm not holding back." So he knew what I was doing.

"Good." I stand now, not wanting to spend any more time here than necessary. "If you hear anything, I expect you to call me," I tell Neill as he shuffles off the couch.

"There's one more thing." He stands. "He had a Northern Ireland accent."

That's the last thing I wanted to hear. "You're positive?" I ask, and he nods. *This isn't good at all.*

I arrive home close to eleven. The house is quiet, but that doesn't mean that everyone is asleep. I find myself upstairs, knocking on Una's door. When I don't get an answer, I enter, but the room is in darkness. The bed is made, and Una isn't here.

I find her in the library, sitting barefoot on a Queen Ann chair. She's twirling a curl around her finger while holding an old paperback in her other hand. I can't read the title, but I can tell she's enjoying it. I'm about to leave when she peeks up from behind the book. Surprise filters through her eyes.

"Don't throw the book at me," I tell her, and she sticks her tongue out, making me smile. Her tongue is really pink, and I'm glad when she puts it back in her pretty mouth. It's tantalizing and distracting.

"I think I will have to start locking my door." Her tone is playful, but I freeze. Does she know that I watch her sleep? I'm not sure what she sees on my face, but she laughs.

"I'm joking. It's just, I'm not a morning person. I had Darragh the other morning, and you this morning."

I relax and enter the room. So the other person was Darragh. He has no respect. "I apologize about Darragh," I tell her as I sit down.

"And who will apologize for you, Shane?" Once again, her tone is playful, but I sense she knows that I watch her.

"I have nothing to apologize for." Her smile slips at my serious words. I don't like sitting here and being questioned, but I don't want to leave her either. Standing, I focus on her, and each step I take closer to her causes a strain on her shoulders.

"I'm going to check your head," I say, and she bends her head for me.

With all her hair, it takes a few seconds to find the cut. The stitches are neatly done. And honestly, there isn't really a reason for me to check it. I rub her hair between my thumb and forefinger. It's extremely soft.

"What are you doing?" Suspicion coats her words.

"I told you, I'm checking your head, so hold still," I tell her. She hadn't moved, but she shifts under my hands. She doesn't like being told what to do.

"It feels like you're touching my hair."

I grin. "I am touching your hair; I have to move it to see the cut."

"It's taking a pretty long time," she huffs, and I can't stop the smile.

"There's a lot of hair to move."

"I'd move a dead body quicker." Her dry comment has me laughing. I don't think she has any idea how ironic it is that she would say that.

"What's so funny?" Darragh comes into the library, and I quickly step away from Una. His smile slips as I stare at him.

"What do you want?"

"I just want to talk to my sister," he says, jutting out his chin. I want to scream at him that she's not his fucking sister. If she was, then she would be my sister, and that was too messed up.

"I want a word," I tell him, leaving the library. I don't turn to see if he follows. I know he will.

He has the sense to close the library door as he leaves. I stop two doors down from it, not able to contain myself.

"She's off-limits from now on," I say. Darragh opens his mouth to speak, but I click my fingers in warning. "I don't care what Liam said. I don't care what you feel or think. She is off-limits."

He's shaking his head. "Why do you even care?" he asks, but he takes a step back while he speaks.

"Because father has left her in my hands, and I'm not a fuckup like you." I can see I've hurt him. Darragh takes another step back.

"Don't forget, Shane, you're not Liam in his eyes either." I hide all emotion at his words, but it stings. It's always been there. I know Liam is the next in line to take father's place, not me.

But when I was younger, it never bothered me to support my brother. I knew he was more vicious than me. He was more controlled when he needed to be, and he could lose control when he needed to as well. My emotions played too heavily into my actions.

Darragh hasn't taken two more steps when the door opens and Una steps out. I can tell from her red cheeks that she's all fired up. Darragh doesn't even stop when she speaks.

"How dare you," Una says. "I can talk to whomever I want. You or your father can't make decisions like that for me."

I glance at Darragh's receding back, his words about Liam still stinging me.

"I'm speaking to you, Shane."

I snap my gaze to Una. I can't do this. "Go back in and read your book," I tell her, expecting her to do as I say, but her dry laugh reminds me she isn't like other people.

"If I had the book, I'd throw it at you right now." Her words are said with hands on her hips. "That was a horrible thing to say to Darragh."

Now I'm starting to question her anger. "Which part?" I offer through clenched teeth.

"You're a piece of work." She shakes her head and storms back into the library. But I can't let it go. It's starting to sound like she has feelings for Darragh.

I'm right behind her. "Why are you getting so mad over Darragh?" I question, and she swings around.

"What are you trying to imply?" Her hands have returned to her hips, but I can see the strain in her face as I keep stepping closer to her.

"You're hell-bent on defending Darragh. Now that I think about it, you spend a lot of time together."

Her face blazes at my accusation, but she takes a step closer to me and pokes me in the chest. "He's my brother." She pokes me a second time. "He treats me with more kindness than you could ever muster up, Shane." She pokes me again while saying my name.

I move closer, stopping her from poking me. Her hand smashes against my chest.

"He is *not* your brother. I'm not your brother." The moment I say it, I regret it. The hurt that crosses her features has me leaving before I explain to her why I said that.

Vicious

CHAPTER SEVEN

UNA

His broad back fills my vision, and I want to pull all the books from the shelves. I'm angry with myself more than him. I allowed myself to feel for him, when all along, I was a job. His father told him to take care of me. That's the whole reason he went above and beyond to help me.

Tears burn my eyes at how stupid I've been. It was like I had spent my whole childhood and into my twenties craving attention from someone I saw as untouchable. Then he gives me a few hours, and I'm falling at his feet like he's some kind of god. The burn that travels up my neck has me covering my cheeks.

It's the burn of shame. I've been such a fool. He must be laughing at me. I don't allow the tears to fall. I'm stronger than this. I leave the library, and with each step, I want to defy him. No one has any right to tell me what to do or who I can hang out with. I go to the bar, knowing that's where I'll find Darragh. He's smiling when he sees me.

"I knew you couldn't resist the dark side." He pours me out a shot of vodka, and I stamp to the bar.

"I'm so fucking angry," I tell him and take the shot. It burns my throat, but it does nothing to quench the fire that's burning in my veins.

"Wow," Darragh yelps while he slaps the bar. "I knew redheads were fiery." He refills the shot glasses, and we both take them at the same time. "Let it out," he tells me, refilling the shot glass again.

"I don't think I could ever let out all the anger I'm feeling right now." Darragh refills his shot glass and downs it.

"He's a dick. Don't let him get to you." Darragh comes around from behind the bar and puts his arm around me. "Fuck him, Una. It's Shane. Just like it's Liam. They aren't like us. We're free," he tells me with a smile before pouring himself out another shot and placing the one I haven't drank in mine. "To freedom," he says, holding up his glass, but I can't drink to that.

"We aren't free, Darragh," I say quietly, because it's true. I'm caught up in what my mother wants me to be. And Darragh is being pushed into a box he refuses to stay in, yet no one is listening to us.

"I don't think I like it when you're acting like a Debbie downer." Darragh drinks his shot, then takes mine out of my hand and drinks it. And just like that, because I'm not partying, I'm not wanted.

My temper flares, and I swing around in the chair, grabbing the bottle of vodka. When I hold it up, Darragh smiles, placing the two shot glasses on the bar. I fill them but don't let him take his. "You answer a question, and then you take a drink," I tell him.

"And what, I ask you a question and then you drink?" He's smirking.

"Yeah," I agree, and he rubs his hands together.

I go first. "Why don't you stand up to Shane?"

"What the fuck kind of question is that?" Darragh is as volatile as me. I smile to ease the tension.

"Do you want a drink or not?" I say, and that does it. He settles.

"I'm only here as long as he allows it," he answers, and I don't even get that, but he knocks back the shot, and I remember that it's his turn to ask me a question.

"Do you have a boyfriend?" His question surprises me.

"No." I drink my shot. "What do you mean you're only here as long as he allows it?"

Darragh refills both shot glasses. "He doesn't like me, and if he had his way, I would be gone." He drinks his shot.

"You don't really believe that?" I question, and he grins.

"That's a second question, and it's my turn."

I reel in my irritation.

"When was the last time you slept with someone?"

"You get to ask me anything, and that's what you ask me?"

Darragh grins. "That's my question."

I roll my eyes. "About three months," I answer honestly, and he hoots while slapping the bar.

"Three months," he roars like I said three years. I knock the shot back.

"What do Shane's tattoos mean?" I ask. The moment it's out of mouth, I can see the wheels turning in Darragh's head.

"This is starting to sound like it's all about Shane."

My heart starts to pound, and I force a laugh while refilling the shot glasses. "It doesn't matter, then. It was a stupid question." I take a shot and Darragh rises.

"He's a prick, Una." The way he says it has me nodding at him. His fists are clenched.

"I know," I answer weakly.

"You're such a fucking liar." He storms from the room, and I feel terrible.

I shouldn't have started this stupid game. It was selfish of me.

I take a swig from the bottle and chase after Darragh. My feet aren't as steady as I expect, but I catch myself before I stumble.

"Darragh." It doesn't seem to matter how many times I call him. He won't stop. It's not until he goes into sittingroom the and sits down that I can see his face.

"I'm sorry," I tell him, knowing quizzing him about Shane wasn't right. "I was curious…"

"Liar." He's shouting again, and I'm questioning if following Darragh was the right thing to do. I want to tell him to calm down, but something is stopping me. "It's always: get close to Darragh to get close to Shane or Liam. Keep Darragh quiet. People can hear him. Hide him away, so no one can see him. I'm fucking sick of it."

I'm frozen as he takes his anger out on a wooden chair, smashing it to pieces. Violence isn't something I've ever been around. Darragh's anger has me rooted to the spot. "I see how you look at him. You have since we were small. You look at him like he's a fucking god." He's too close for comfort, and I step away from Darragh. He throws his head back and really laughs.

"Go on, sweetheart, run back to your prince. You have no idea who he is."

I want to shout at him to tell me, but speaking doesn't seem like the best idea. He's staring at me, and it's like someone snaps their fingers, and he's Darragh again.

"Jesus, Una, I'm sorry."

I'm shaking my head, trying to tell him it's fine.

"You're as white as a ghost. I've really fucking scared you." My heart is still pounding, but my muscles relax slightly as Darragh steps away from me and sits on the couch.

"It's obviously something you need to talk about," I say from the same spot.

Darragh is sitting down and pours white powder onto the small coffee table. He uses a card and cuts the cocaine up. "Nah, it is what it is."

Clearly not, I think, but I don't voice this as he rolls up a fifty and uses it to snort the powder up his nose. As he sits back, he inhales deeply before lying back into the couch.

"Want to go to a party?" He's up now, rubbing his nose. "Have some," he says, pointing at the two white lines that are still on the table.

"No, I'm fine," I tell him, and he shrugs before snorting up the other two lines. Watching him, I see how far he's gone. Does his family see how damaged he is?

"Your nose is bleeding, Darragh." My heart is heavy for him, but he grins and goes to the bathroom. While he's gone, I start to tidy up the smashed chair. He's going to get himself in trouble with that temper, or God forbid, hurt someone or himself.

"Do you want me to get Finn for you?" I know they're close, and I don't want to be around Darragh, but leaving him alone isn't a good idea either.

"He's off duty tonight. Don't worry, Una, you can go. You don't have to stay." He lights up a fag, and there's so much wrong with that sentence, but I wouldn't know where to start.

I don't move, and I can see the irritation in his shoulders. "What are you still doing here?" As he blows smoke into the air, he focuses on the floor to the left of my foot. *This is Darragh,* I tell myself. *I have nothing to fear. We all lose our cool now and again.*

"Where's the party?" I ask. He grins, and now, so do I.

"Let's party," he tells me, throwing the fag into the pool. We leave, and I don't allow myself to think. I get into his car with him.

I'm not sure how we make it safely, but we do. I'm still pumped from the speed the car was going and from the near misses. I'm not an adrenaline junkie, but the vodka and rush has me alive as Darragh and I get out of the car.

The party is a rave, and it's being held in an exhibition center in Navan. Its beat can be heard from where we parked, which is like the size of three soccer fields away. From the moment we step out of the vehicle, the party has started. There are people everywhere. Laughing, drinking, making out, getting sick, and even having sex. Yeah, there seem to be no boundaries.

"Darragh." Brian moves toward us, saying Darragh's name in a deep voice. They embrace, and when Brian notices me, he winks.

"Red. You came back for seconds," he says. He reeks of cologne and alcohol, but those blue eyes are a vortex.

"I didn't realize I had firsts, blondie," I tell him, and he grins, handing me a bottle of something. I take it, and it burns. Whiskey, I think. When I cough, the two girls behind him giggle. They both wear bikini tops and short denim skirts. I'm overdressed in jeans and a jumper, but I'm not here to get laid. Brian hasn't taken his eyes off me, and I start to question what exactly happened between us.

"What was the stuff you gave me the other night?" I ask, and he throws his arm around my neck as we walk toward the rave. I glance back to see Darragh with an arm around each girl.

"You want some more, red?"

I glare sideways at Brian and shrug his arm off me. He's hot and all, but something about him isn't right. "No, I'll pass. And stop calling me red," I tell him, and he laughs at me like I'm a little child having a cute tantrum.

"Find me later when you mellow out." He walks on into a crowd and greets some guy with a shaved head. I give his back the fingers.

"Come on, play nice." Darragh's beside me with a blonde under each arm. They smile in unison at me.

I give Darragh a fake smile. "This is me playing nice."

We get split up the moment we enter the rave. The heat has started a coat of sweat over my body. My skin is itchy and tight as I push through and make my way to the bar. Drink is slopped everywhere, and my top soaks up some from the counter.

"A large vodka," I roar at the barman. He has one of those really big ear piercings that must be painful.

"Mixer?" he shouts back, and I shake my head. He pushes a pint of pure vodka toward me, and I pay a twenty for it. I don't mind. I stand at the bar and drink the whole lot while holding my nose the whole time. When it's gone, I'm not yet out of it enough to join everyone around me as they move to the music.

Whatever pumps through their bodies has them in their own little world. I want to be in mine. The heat has the air hot, and I pull off my jumper. My pink bra blends in with all the multitude of colored bras that flash around me. Wrapping my jumper around my waist, I move through the crowd. Warm flesh pushes against mine, most of it wet with sweat, and there's something freeing about it. Closing my eyes, I let the beat take over, and the vodka fully enters my blood stream.

When I open my eyes, Brian is there, and I smile as he wraps his strong arms around me. His mouth goes to my neck, and I wrap my arms around it, pulling him closer.

"I was searching for you," he whispers in my ear, and my smile widens.

"Yeah?" My word slurs, dragging out at the end. I try to make myself more alert, but I'm cocooned in heat and bodies, and now Brian. I don't want the world to come back into focus.

When his tongue finds its way into my mouth, I don't stop him, not even when the sizzle of something on my tongue reminds me of the last time I kissed him. I swallow the tablet, and when Brian moves away, I allow the music and drugs to take me.

Lights burn my eyes, and I move away. "Get up, Una." Brian is there. Why does my face sting? Grass is under my hands. The music pounds behind me. I must be outside. Lights are still shining, burning me.

"Knock off the headlights." Brian is shouting, and the light vanishes.

My body bounces up and down. "Put her top on." I'm sure

that's Darragh's voice. The vehicle moves under me. I can smell smoke. Trying to sit up has me falling over, and someone laughs. I join in their laughter.

The car stops, and a door slams. "Hurry the fuck up." It's Darragh's voice again.

"Brian, put her top on. How many more times do I have to fucking say it?" I'm dragged roughly off the floor of the car, and my stomach hurls.

"Open the door quick." I'm pushed out onto gravel as my stomach empties all over my hands.

"I'm so fucking dead." I'm not sure who's speaking. Darkness moves in along the edges of my vision.

CHAPTER EIGHT

SHANE

It's one in the morning when I leave Dad and Liam. I've informed them of everything I found out about the new supplier. Dad wants me to take a step back from it until we find out exactly who this person is. Anyone crossing over the border isn't someone we want to get tangled up in.

I understand what he's saying, but to me, this is a different time. We should attack first, not sit back and wait to be attacked. This is our turf, and I'm not letting it go. I don't care about the cost.

But we have more problems. It seems to be coming from all sides. Liam met with all the brothels in the area, and there's a huge demand for virgins, which we can't seem to meet. It isn't my problem, and I'm pretty confident that Liam is capable of handling it.

I find myself outside Una's door again, and a part of me knows I should stop this. I hurt her so much today, and maybe that's all I will ever do to her. I rest my head against her door as I try to talk myself into going to bed. She's asleep, and if I keep sneaking into her room, I'll get caught.

No matter the thoughts that go through my head, I find myself opening the bedroom door. I'm not sure how I feel when I see her bed made. She isn't here. Maybe she returned to reading her book. I need to give her some space. I return to my own room and climb into bed.

I wake up and check my phone. It's four in the morning. I'll kill Darragh. I climb out of bed and peer out the window. My room overlooks the courtyard. I see Darragh's car parked out back. Another one has arrived, the noise and rattles of a hole in the exhaust bangs away until they park. The people in the car climb out, and I get back into bed. Once they are all in the pool house, the noise disappears.

I'm out of bed again as my stomach tightens, and I find myself at Una's door, pushing it open. I curse. Her bed is empty. I return to my room and get on a T-shirt, jeans, and this time, I put on shoes and socks and make my way to the pool house. The closer I get, the clearer the noise of music and laughter is.

I open the door and am surprised to see Brian here with Darragh. Both of them cheer when they see me, like they've been awaiting my arrival. My eyes skim the two half-naked girls as I search for Una. Fear tightens like a fist in my stomach.

"Where is she?" I'm in front of Darragh, and it's taking everything not to kill him.

"Shane?" The bathroom door has opened, and Una is standing in the doorway. She tilts her head and furrows her brows in complete confusion at seeing me. My heart pounds in my chest as I take her in.

"I told you to put her top back on."

My head snaps to Darragh, and with narrowed eyes, I give him his last warning. If I don't leave now, I will kill him.

Everyone is silent.

"Put your clothes on," I tell Una quietly and stop staring at her chest. It takes a lot of my willpower. Her eyes are dilating rapidly; whatever she took is still in her system. I'm not sure if she heard me. Her mouth moves like she's trying to form a word, and I cross the room and pick her up. She gives a little squeal as I carry her out of the pool house. The air is cold on her bare skin, which I'm trying not to stare at.

But Una is lying back in my arms, her head thrown back, a smile on her face. But I don't feel like smiling. I don't know what's happening to her. She never used to be like this. She was outgoing, wild in a way, but not going out and doing drugs. I won't allow myself to think about why she is half-dressed. I can't.

"Brian." I tighten my grip on her as she calls his name, and instead of thinking about her calling another man, I keep moving forward. My sole focus is on each step I take as I climb the stairs.

Una stirs, pulling herself closer to my chest as she tightens her arms around my neck. I wish I could take the steps two at a time. Her breath on my neck and the soft flesh against any available skin I have on display is driving me mad. I make it to the landing when she speaks again after inhaling deeply.

"Shane." My pulse speeds up as she says my name, and I shush her. Her chest vibrates with laughter. "Still telling me what to do."

She leans out so she can stare at me, and I'm surprised at how alert she is. Small marks are on her cheek, like she was scraped. I want to run my fingers along the area and remove the marks from her skin. I'm close to my room, and I carry her into it.

"You won't listen, Una," I say back, and she smiles at me, her eyes staring at my lips.

"You're gorgeous, Shane."

I stop walking and stare at her. For a moment, she's sober and knows what she is saying, and that's how she really sees me. But reality kicks in, and I snap my gaze away from her smiling face and carry her into my bathroom. She has her own in her room, but I haven't a clue where anything is.

I slowly lower her down onto the closed toilet, and she becomes intrigued with her surroundings. "Will you stay here for a second?" I ask her, and her eyes rest on me. She nods but doesn't speak. I quickly grab a T-shirt, and she is still sitting on the toilet when I come back in. She doesn't object as I carefully put it on her.

Her eyes never leave my face. No one can make me as unsettled as Una does. A smile grows on her face, and she reaches out and embraces my face. I'm frozen.

"I've crushed on you for so long." The confession is said with a small laugh, and I want to hear this, but the drugs are making her talk crazy.

"Let me check your face," I say to her, leaning away from her hand so I can get some disinfectant wipes. She doesn't move. Her eyes flutter closed as I return.

I dab the area, and her eyes shoot open. "I'm sorry," I tell her as she bites her lip.

"You were untouchable to me. So out of my league." Once again, I focus on cleaning her face. She's distracting, and it's taking all my willpower not to listen to her words. She laughs softly again, and when I flicker my gaze to hers, her eyes are glistening.

"You'll just keep hurting me, and I'll keep letting you." I don't have a clue what she's talking about, but her eyes are filling up, and I'm not sure what to do.

"You need to wash your arms, Una," I tell her, and she nods. She seems more together, and I leave the bathroom and sit on my bed. I don't leave the bedroom in case she needs me.

Taking out my phone, I ring Finn. It's close to five in the morning, but he answers. "You need to get home and sort Darragh out," I tell him, expecting him to do as I say. What I don't expect is for Finn to say no. Now isn't the time for him to grow a pair of balls.

"How would you like for me to reunite Siobhan with her aunt?" I stand. I don't need his back talk. "I don't care about her. I'll make it so fucking slow. Now get your ass over here and sort

Darragh out, and I want Brian off my property too." I hang up and sit back down. I need to calm down before I go down and sort it out myself.

The bathroom door opens, and my head snaps up. Una is standing there, one arm behind the door. She looks so good in my green T-shirt. That's all she's wearing. I swallow as my eyes drink in the sight of her. She's in my room—how many times have I fantasized about her? She takes a step toward me, and I grip the blanket under my hands. She isn't thinking straight, but I can't find the words to stop her as she advances toward me.

She reaches me, and I settle my hands on her hips, stopping her from moving any closer. "Una, you don't want to do this," I tell her quietly. Her skin burns under my hands, and I'm losing the ability to stop this as she easily moves forward. I release her as she straddles me. I keep my eyes closed at the contact and breathe her in.

"Una." I say her name as I grip the quilts. This is wrong, but her body this close to mine feels so right. When her hands grip my shoulders, I allow my eyes to reach hers.

"I want this, Shane," she tells me.

My heart pounds, and I release the quilt and flip her around until she's under me. Her eyes are wide, her chest moving quickly, and I'm waiting for her to say no. I'm searching her face for a sign that I need to stop this, but she reaches up and caresses my face, her body pushing against mine. I can't stop the moan that escapes my lips.

Her hands direct my face closer to hers. I can't stop staring at her. I can't stop this. I'm falling too deep, and I don't think I can climb back out. Her breath brushes against my lips, and everything in my body jerks. She will undo me, and I want her to, but not like this. When my forehead touches hers, I try to calm my pounding heart.

"Una," I say her name, and it's what gives me the strength to pull back. I remove her hands from my face, and already, I can see the damage my actions are causing. I'm shaking my head, searching for the right words.

Her eyes grow wider, her nostrils flare, and she's wriggling under me. "Let me up." Her voice is rising, and I don't release her. She's too angry, and when she's angry, she seems to do stupid things.

"Let me up, Shane. I'm going back to the party. Brian will give me what I want."

I push her hands above her head, my anger at her words barely containable. The air is sucked out of the room. I'm searching her face, but she's grinning at me like this is one big fucking joke.

"What do you want?" I shout, and her grin slips, but I can't figure her out. She wriggles, and I push my body harder against hers.

"You will answer me," I demand, and her eyes flare to life. I know I've pushed too hard; now she'll push back.

"Not this," she tells me, and I'm off her in a second, imagining what she must think of me.

"I'm sorry," I tell her. I want to pull down my T-shirt so it covers her legs, but I don't dare move as she sits up on my bed.

She wraps her arms around her waist as if she has a pain in her stomach, and I take a step closer to her. Her head whips up at my movement, and she raises a hand.

"I'm going to bed. Don't you dare follow me." She rises, holds her head high, and walks out of my room. I count to ten before I follow her. I check to make sure she does go into her bedroom. She slams the door. She has some temper. I don't know what to do. I can't stand in the hall all day and night and guard her. It's been a long time since I felt this close to snapping. I leave my room and make my way to the gym, which is located in the basement. I need some sort of release, and violence will have to do.

Vicious

CHAPTER NINE

O'REAGAN
AN CHLANN

UNA

I wake with a sore head. My cheek stings as I brush it off the pillow while turning. As I slowly sit up, I try to remember how I got to bed last night. My clothes send alarm bells ringing in my head. It's not that they're nonexistent. Instead, I'm in a man's T-shirt. I quickly snap my gaze to the left side of the bed, but no one is there. While hanging out over the bed, I scan the floor for anything to suggest what happened last night, but there are no clues.

Dancing at a rave—I remember that. Brian. I groan as I slowly begin to remember the rave and the car drive home. It's all foggy like a dream, but I know it happened. A squeal leaves me as I start to also remember Shane. "Nooooo," I cover my mouth, trying to push last night's words back down my throat.

The burn of humiliation has me burying my head in my quilt. "Noooo," I growl into the quilt. I told him that I liked him. I said he was a god. I tried to seduce him. Right now, I want my brain to short-circuit. He turned me down. Oh, God. This is humiliating. I can never face him again. I try to calm myself by taking deep breaths.

It's okay. He'll avoid me like the plague. He won't want to be around a desperado. Oh, God. I told him I wanted to sleep with him. I bury my head deeper in my blanket. The burn on my face isn't lessening. It's spreading to my whole body. I want to die. I think dying from humiliation is possible.

"Good morning."

I freeze, holding my breath, and I hope I'm still remembering. I'm praying that Shane isn't the one saying good morning to me. I can't cope. I slowly raise my head and yelp when I my gaze lands on him, standing in my bedroom. Shane is fresh and clean and gorgeous in tan trousers and a black fleece jumper. I'm on fire with embarrassment.

"Can't you knock?" I shout while pointing at my door. I want him to disappear. I can't deal with this.

"I did. Several times," he answers dryly. My hands grip the end of the T-shirt that I'm twisting in knots under the quilt. Then I remember it's Shane's top, and I release it quickly as a new burn erupts across my face, traveling all the way up to the tips of my ears.

"Fine, what do you want?" I want this to be quick. Like pulling off a bandage. I imagine an apology is in order for throwing myself at him. I hope not, but if it ends this torture, I'm willing to consider it.

"You have work in thirty minutes. You've been slacking off since you arrived here. So you either meet me in the kitchen in fifteen, or you can pack your belongings and go home."

I'm stunned momentarily. What the hell is his game? He can't kick me out. But then I see that he wants me to run home with my tail between my legs. He might not like me, but I swallow the humiliation that burns through me. I keep eye contact as I throw the covers back and am glad when his jaw clenches. A reaction.

"I'll be down in fifteen," I tell him as I stroll past him. I'm not sure how the hell my legs are carrying me as I go into my wardrobe. It's there I tell myself to breathe as I gather fresh clothes with trembling hands. When I return, Shane is gone, and I let out a shaky breath.

As I enter the kitchen, I'm repeating a mantra in my head that Shane isn't there. But everything is working against me. He's there on his phone. My attention snaps to Mary, who smiles at me, but it fades as her eyes roam my face. "What happened now, Una?"

Shane clears his throat, and I keep my back to him. "Me being drunk and stupid last night. I fell on the gravel."

Mary inspects me closer, and I want to tell her to leave it, but she's always been a mammy to us when we're here. Well, to some of us.

"You cleaned it out?" she asks. Shane clears his throat again, and I'm tempted to offer him a glass of water.

"Yes," is all I say before sitting down the furthest away from Shane as I can. I don't glance up to see if he's watching me, but I sense his eyes on me. His hands were gentle while cleaning my face last night. If I keep this up, I'll be permanently red. I remind myself that I am stronger than this. So he turned me down. I need to get over it already.

"Two fried eggs and one piece of bacon?" Mary asks once I'm seated.

"Yes, that's perfect. Thanks, Mary." She turns back to the pan, and I focus on the fixture and fittings of the kitchen.

It has every mod con a kitchen can have. An island that can seat six dominates the large space. A breakfast bar runs half the length of the kitchen, separating the cooking area from the dining area, where I'm sitting. I'm a bit overenthusiastic when Finn arrives in, but sitting in silence with Shane is painful.

"Good morning, Finn. I haven't seen much of you," I say, and he grabs a banana and starts peeling it as he makes his way over to the table and sits beside me.

"Yeah, I've been busy." Shane clears his throat again, and Finn and I are on the same page as we both ignore him.

"What happened to your face?" He takes a huge bite of the banana as he speaks.

"What happened your face?" I throw back. *Lord, it's a scratch.*

He holds his hands up. "Hungover, are we?"

"Sorry. Yeah, a bit. But don't tell anyone," I say with a grin, and he smirks.

"Where's your other half?"

Now Finn isn't smiling. "In bed sleeping off the mother of all hangovers."

"Are you not going to greet me, brother?" Shane asks as Mary places my breakfast in front of me. Everyone's attention falls on Shane, and the tension in the room seems to grow. Mary shuffles back to the stove, and I start to eat. I'm not hungry, but I don't know what else to do.

"Why should I? You threatened Siobhan." Siobhan is Finn's new girlfriend, and from the sounds of it, their relationship is serious. But to hear that Shane threatened her has me raising an eyebrow at him. His jaw is clenched, and he flickers a glance at Finn and away from my questioning stare.

"Don't be so petty. It was a few words."

A vein is flickering like a heartbeat in Finn's neck. "No, it wasn't. You know what you said, and I'm not having it." Mary puts a fry in front of Finn, and he quickly thanks her.

"What are you going to do?" Shane is leaning forward, and there's something in his stance that tells me this is far more serious than it appears to be.

Finn has a death grip on his knife and fork. They appear as deadly weapons now. His nostrils flare as he stares down at Shane, and he looks like he wants to hurt him. But Shane's eyes are shining with violence. It's like he's excited at the idea of hurting Finn.

I want to defuse the situation, so I do the one thing I can think of. I knock my coffee over with a little more force than intended. I wanted to send the coffee pouring over the side, but the mug goes too, smashing into pieces on the floor. All eyes are on me.

"Sorry, my hand slipped," I say, getting up. Shane stares at me, and I'm not sure if he's mad or what he's thinking.

"I'll get it. Una, finish your breakfast." Mary is there with a cloth, but I start picking up pieces of the mug.

"Una, leave it alone before you cut yourself." Shane's words are barked at me, and I'm close to losing it with him.

I take the cloth off Mary. "Please, Mary, I'll clean it up." She gives me a nod before leaving me.

"Mary, clean it up." Shane stops her in her tracks, and I grind my teeth. He's controlling. I gather up the rest of the mug and stand.

"Mary, it's done. Seriously, it's fine." She's waiting for Shane's word, and he nods at her to go back to the kitchen. I'm shaking my head in disgust at him. I really want to throw the broken mug at him, but I can't. Michael picks that moment to enter the kitchen, and he smiles when he sees us all.

"Ah, I was wondering where everyone was." He stops me as I make my way to the bin and kisses the top of my head. When he sees the broken mug in my hand, he leans out. "Be careful not to cut yourself."

"That's what I said," Shane chimes in from the corner like I'm some fragile little flower.

"It's a mug. Not a sword." Michael doesn't appreciate my smart mouth, but lets me pass as he sits down.

I'm ready to return to the table and eat my breakfast when Shane stands up all cheery. "Are you ready to start work, Una?" he asks me like we're best pals. I narrow my focus at my breakfast, and Shane flashes a glance at his watch. "If you need more time?"

I wave his comment away. I'm hungry, but I'll be dammed if I ask for more time. "No. I'm good to go."

"I'm very proud of you." Michael's words cause a swell to rise in my chest and deflate, leaving a sense of tightness behind. My father always told me he was proud of me. Whether I made a daisy chain or passed exams, he was there raising me up. Swallowing the lump, I tighten my lips before nodding.

"Thanks," I tell him and quickly leave the warmth of the kitchen. My mother never told me she was proud of me. If I really think about it, I was always a disappointment. I never stuck to anything, and she hated it.

She enrolled me in Irish dancing, which lasted a week. Drama class lasted a day. Football ended up being the longest, lasting three months, but she pulled me from the team saying it was too boyish. I hated piano. The violin—someone shoot me. I tried many things but hated them all. The first time I fell in love with something was on my sixteenth birthday, when Shane bought me the horse. The happy memory dissolves as Shane walks ahead of me in wellies.

"What are you doing?" I try to catch up with him. Panic is making me stand in his path.

"I'm going to work?" He walks around me, and I'm standing there stumped but soon catch up with him. Working with Shane isn't a good idea. "I'm fine with Stephen, Shane. I seriously don't need you babysitting me."

"You needed me last night." His smartass words have me storming ahead of him.

"No, I didn't. You needed me to need you last night. That's why you arrived like some avenging angel." I'm talking through my ass, but I haven't a clue what to do. When I look back at Shane, his jaw is clenched like I've really hit a nerve, and I think, *Good.*

I check the area but can't see Stephen. I start to call him but get no answer.

"I told him he could have the day off," Shane informs me. When I flicker a gaze at him, he's leaning against the wall, staring at me as I run around like a headless chicken.

"So, what, you're working with me today?"

Now he smirks, and it isn't a nice one. "No, you're working. I'm overseeing."

I could walk away, as this is just a game to him, but I have my pride, and I'm not afraid of work. I get my gloves on and start at the first stable. Wheeling up the barrow, I then leave it outside the stable as I shovel it out. Once I have that done, I fill it with fresh straw and remove any strands of loose straw from the drinking sink in the corner.

Shane does as he promises. He watches me—or oversees things, as he put it. I remove my jacket as I get to the fifth stall and start again.

"What is your job?" I ask him. May as well have someone to talk to. The farm brings in most of their income, but when I really think about it, I never see any of the boys working around the farm.

"The family business." Shane's answer captures my attention, and I stop working and rest on the shovel. I push hair out of my face. I tied it up earlier, but some curls have managed to burst free and find their way into my eyes.

"Which is what? The farm? I never see you do any work."

Shane stares at me. It's unsettling, but I hold my ground firmly. "We have other businesses," he answers, and I can see this will be like trying to get blood from a stone. I return to work.

"It isn't exactly above board," he adds. I narrow my eyes at Shane. His look of innocence causes a smile of surprise to spread rapidly across my face.

"An upstanding citizen like you, Shane? Never," I joke, and his lips tug up, sending my stomach erupting with butterflies. Butterflies that I want to crush under my wellies. They have no business being here anymore. That ship has sailed.

"I don't think you would approve, Una, if you knew." He lowers his lashes as he speaks, but his smile is gone, and I'm taking a step closer to him. Now I want to know.

"Maybe I will," I tell him seriously, and his lashes rise. He's studying me carefully, making an assessment to find out how serious I am.

"Let's just say it isn't legal."

His answer has me rolling my eyes. "That's just like saying it isn't above board. It means the same thing. So all of you work in the unsavory business section?" I say unsavory with air quotes, and Shane smiles at me.

"You could say that."

"I could say a lot of things," I mumble under my breath and return to work, but from his soft laugh, I know he heard me.

"We need to talk about last night."

That's the last thing I want to talk about. "No, we don't," I tell him. I glance up as the straw crunches behind me.

"We do," he says, way too close to me, and I need to save face.

I take a deep breath and turn around. My pulse spikes at his closeness. "I had too much drink on me. I have needs, and you where there." Heat rushes across my face, but I hold eye contact.

"That's all it was?" he questions, and I can hear the control in his words. I'm searching his face. My heart is ready to leave my chest.

"I don't know why you came down there and got me. I can't make sense of it." I turn the whole thing on him, hoping to deflect from my embarrassing behavior.

"You had no idea where you were. You were half-naked, Una. Hanging out with a bunch of lowlifes." He stuffs his hands into his fleece pockets roughly, like if he doesn't, he might strangle me.

"I'm sorry you don't approve of who I hang out with. But let me remind you that one of those lowlifes is your brother, and Brian is nice." Okay, that last part is a lie, but I can see it's winding him up.

"Brian is nice? He's a scumbag. You should be thanking me for coming down there and getting you."

I laugh with anger. "Or what, Shane? God forbid I enjoyed myself."

"With Brian? You were mumbling his name."

I want to wipe the smirk off his face. "I was mumbling lots of stupid things." I'm breathing heavy, and I don't want this conversation anymore. I go to leave, but Shane stands in my way. His hands are lost at his side. When I raise my lashes and gaze up at him, I can see he's working a muscle in his jaw. He's no longer smiling.

"Did you mean anything you said?" His brows are furrowed; there's something vulnerable in how he's looking at me. My heart kicks up a notch, and I'm confused.

I'm not sure if I want to hurt him or be honest. But being honest seems to lead to one road, and that's hurt. "I was just looking for some fun."

He lowers his lashes and gives a quick nod before he peers back up. His brown eyes appear almost black as he stares at me.

"It's lunchtime," he tells me, and I stare after him as he walks back toward the house. Something is sitting on my chest, and I can't breathe. Drops land on my cheek. I'm crying. I stay in the stall and cry. I'm not sure why, exactly. It isn't like he cares. *So why did he look so hurt?* But goddamn it, he hurt me.

CHAPTER TEN

O'REAGAN
AN CHLANN

UNA

I'm not a girl who cries over boys. This isn't me. But deep down, I know this is more than a crush. This has been years in the making. I didn't think it would end like this. Tears keep falling without my permission, and I wipe them away angrily. I leave the stables and make my way to the ones that the livestock are being held in. There, I find my horse. She's not as jumpy, and she lets me rub her straight away.

"Una."

I inwardly scream leave me alone, but it's Finn, and Finn is sweet. I pop my head out of the stall. "I'm here," I tell him with a smile.

His eyebrows dip. "Are you okay?"

Ah, shit. He can see I've been crying. "Yeah, I got some dung in my eye," I tell him with a wave of my hand. But the O'Reagans are always hands-on, and Finn is holding my face. He's taller than me—all the boys are—so he's looking into my eye.

"Don't blink," he tells me while stretching my eye slightly, and I can't stop blinking.

"I don't see anything," he says, but he still hasn't released me.

"Must be gone," I tell him, and he steps back.

I rub my eye to add to my story. "Yeah, it's a bit sore, but I think I'm good."

He smiles. "I thought, for a second, that Shane had upset you. He has a habit of upsetting people."

"I see that. He sure upset you," I say, closing the stall. "When am I going to get to meet Siobhan?" I add before looking at him. I don't want to talk about Shane and me. Our names being uttered in the same sentence does something funny to my heart.

"Soon, I hope. We'll organize something."

I smile genuinely. "I'd really like that."

"I've been sent out to get you for dinner."

"I'm not hungry."

Finn shrugs apologetically. "Dad's orders."

Well, I can't say no to Michael. When we arrive inside, I wash up before going to the main dining room where everyone is sitting. A seat is vacant between Shane and Liam, and the seat is pulled out for me already. I sit down with dread as I face Darragh, who winks at me. Michael nods in approval, and Mary starts to bring in steaming plates of dinner.

"How's your eye?" Finn asks, and I want to kick him for directing all attention on me.

"What happened?" Shane, the caveman, is sitting forward, looking ready to start a war.

"My eye is fine, Finn. Thanks so much for asking." He gives me an apologetic smile at my sarcastic tone.

"I leave you for ten minutes and something happens?" I turn to Shane, because I can't believe his attitude.

"Yes, you're right, Shane. Where would I be without my

knight in shining armor? I suppose you would have deflected the lump of dung and stopped it from hitting my eye."

Darragh snorts, and Liam shifts beside me. I turn to him, and I swear Liam's eyebrow rises slightly, but I could be wrong. Shane, on the other hand, is angry. His face is tight, and he gives me a quick nod.

"There's no need for such hostility," Michael says, and I remember my manners and that I'm in someone else's home, and fighting with his son isn't nice. Michael isn't looking at me. He looks at everyone as he speaks. But his words are for me. I am being hostile.

"I'm sorry, Michael. I'm tired and cranky," I say against every fiber in my body, and Michael seems pleased. Mary has set a plate in front of everyone, and when I stare forward, Darragh is still smiling and mouths, "Woman things" to me. I give him a glare of pure disgust.

Michael says a short prayer to God over the food before we start eating. I'm starving, and the roast dinner is divine. I pour more gravy over my spuds, and when I glance up, Michael is smiling. "Nothing as nice as seeing a girl *really* eat."

I smile at him, not sure if that was really a compliment. I dig back in to my food when he returns to his. Shane's arm keeps brushing mine, and I flicker a quick glance at him. His face is serious, but his movements seem intentional.

"Your mother rang," Michael kicks off, and I freeze, my fork held in midair. My eyes shoot to Darragh, then to Finn as they glance at me and then at Michael. I put the fork in my mouth and chew the food that has turned to lead.

"She's worried about you," Michael continues. Now I'm questioning if that's what this dinner is about. And she isn't worried about me; she's worried about what the neighbors will think when I'm not around. Or what my work must be saying since I never arrived in. Or what college is saying. That's what she cares about, not me.

I pour more gravy over my food. "Anyone want some?" I offer. Darragh and Finn are shaking their heads, trying not to make eye contact with me. Like I might freak out any second.

I offer some to Liam, and he meets my eye. "Please. Just on the carrots." Odd, but okay. I pour until he tells me to stop. I don't want to turn to Shane and Michael, but I have to.

"Gravy?" I ask Shane, and his eyes have softened for the first time since he left me in the stables. I don't need his pity. He nods his head, and I pour nearly half the jug over Shane's food.

Michael is peering up at me, and I hate it. I don't offer him gravy. I hate that he brought her up. He was married to her. He divorced her because he knew how she was.

No one speaks to me again as I finish my dinner. But a nice flow of conversation takes over the table. It's about cars, but it's really soothing to hear the boys getting on. Even Liam chimes in, and I try not to stare at him when he laughs. It's not a huge laugh, but it's not a sound I've heard before.

Shane eats his dinner that's soaked in gravy. It must be stomach turning, but he never complains, and I start to shift in my seat at every forkful that enters his mouth. I'm angry because he turned me down, but he doesn't deserve my anger. I try to cheer up as the dessert arrives. It's pavlova and strawberries with cream, and this meal is looking like my favorite food. The lump in my throat is back.

"I bought a bike over the summer," I offer up, trying to join in the conversation.

"Like, with pedals?" Finn says, and I laugh at him. Darragh snorts too, and Shane shakes a little beside me.

"You are so funny. No, with an engine." The room grows serious. I don't need a lecture about safety.

"I have a helmet," I add, and laughter erupts around the table.

"I bet it's a moped," Darragh offers up, and he laughs harder.

"No, it's a scooter," Finn teases.

When I glance up at Michael, he's really smiling. I join the laughter. I love seeing him happy.

"Is it running?" The serious question comes from Liam, and I turn to him.

"No, I was saving up to restore it. But I will get it running," I tell him, and he gives me a nod of what looks like approval.

"What make is it?" Liam is being quite the conversationalist. I'm surprised.

Mary arrives in with teas and coffees, and I thank her before answering. "It's a Honda. Really sweet. It needs a few parts and a bit of a paint job, but then it should be good to go."

"Shane's really good with engines." Darragh gives up this information, and when I glance at Shane from under my lashes, my stomach tightens.

"If you want, I can check it out," he says. My pulse spikes at how he's looking at me.

"Yeah. That would be great," I tell him. This could be a peace offering on both ends.

"I might get a bike too," Darragh says. "We can ride together."

"You'd be dead in a day," Finn tells him. "How many cars have you gone through?"

"A few." Darragh shrugs like it's no big deal.

"Try six. I know because I pay for them." Michael's words have my mouth dropping open.

"Six! You are so spoiled."

"You bought Finn a house. No one's shouting about that," Darragh fires back.

There's an odd silence around the table, but my mind is finding this conversation crazy. He bought Finn a house. What dad does that?

"I bought you one, too," Michael says before taking a forkful of dessert.

I follow suit, taking a bite of my dessert. Darragh's face turns slightly red. Now I question why they live here, if they both have houses. And if they do, there's no doubt that Liam and Shane have their own homes too. But this house is enchanting. I would live here, too.

"You are all spoiled," I say, then shovel a forkful of the most delicious pavlova into my mouth.

"I'm glad someone said it." I grin at Michael, and we finish our desserts. I don't want to leave. Michael chats about his first car, and I love listening to old times. Liam excuses himself and then Finn. Darragh isn't far after, leaving me with Shane and Michael.

"Do you still have the car?" I ask, wanting to see it. It sounds like something from the movies.

"I do. I'll show it to you some day."

I'm smiling. I have a love for old things. I don't know why exactly, but I do.

Shane hasn't said much beside me, and I glance at him to find him watching me with a soft smile on his handsome face. "I wasn't aware you had a love for old cars."

"Yeah, I've always loved Cadillacs and Pontiacs—cars like that."

"You're so like your mother." The softness in Michael's voice surprises me, but I don't like the comparison. I also don't want to spoil the evening.

"She likes cars?" I ask, and Michael laughs.

"No, she wouldn't be able to tell one car from the other. But you have her passion for life. When she talks about something she loves, she lights up, and so do you."

The compliment has me blushing.

"She's a good woman," he adds.

I can now see where this is going. "Is that why you divorced? Because she's such a good woman?" I can't help the scratchy tone to my voice.

Michael lowers his spoon, and already, I want to apologize. "No, your mother and I weren't compatible. That doesn't make her a bad woman, Una." Michael dabs his face with a cloth napkin before excusing himself.

"Sometimes I don't know what's wrong with me," I say to the almost-empty table. I'm waiting for Shane to leave, but he doesn't.

"I think you're hurting."

I glance at him sideways, and he's staring me. "I think so, too." I whisper the truth, and a lump forms in my throat.

"Do you want to talk about it?" There's a gentleness in his tone that nearly undoes me.

"No. Yes." I laugh. "I'm not sure."

CHAPTER ELEVEN

O'REAGAN
AN CHLANN

SHANE

I wait, not speaking, allowing her to make up her own mind. I want her to tell me. I want to know every part of Una, but I won't rush her. She's staring down at her coffee cup, and I take in the beauty of her face. Her lashes lift, and I'm looking into her eyes. My stomach squeezes.

"My looks come from my dad," she says with a sadness tugging at her voice and eyes. She pulls a curl and lets it bounce back. I'm picturing a male version of Una, and I try to imagine her with him. "He got it, you know. He got how it felt to look different." She angles her hand at her eyes.

"He must have been very handsome," I say, and she smiles sweetly. Her head dips, and she rests her face on her hand. She smiles. "I think he was," she tells me. The sadness is still there, but she's smiling.

She glances away and licks her lips, and her brows pull

down. She's so close to crying. "I miss him," she tells the floral wallpaper. I want to reach for her, comfort her, but I wait until she looks at me again.

"What happened?" I asked. I know her dad died when she was young, but I never knew how.

"It was a freak accident. A tree fell, blocking the road. My dad being my dad, tried to clear it." One free tear falls, but she doesn't stop talking as it drops off her chin and onto the table. "Another fell and killed him."

"I'm sorry." I whisper the words, knowing they are meaningless, but she takes my hand in hers.

"It was a long time ago, and I know you lost too. With your mum." I'm nodding, but all the blood has rushed to my hand where she touches me, and I allow myself to touch her back. I rotate my hand until our fingers line up, and I entwine them. Una sits back, slightly startled, but she doesn't pull away.

"Yeah, that should have never happened," I tell our entwined fingers. My mother was far too young to die.

"Did they ever find out who it was?"

I glance up at Una, my focus on her lush lips. She licks them, and my attention is taken with her pink tongue. When it disappears back into her mouth, I speak.

"No, but we will." I stare at her. "I will," I add. My mother was murdered in a drive-by shooting. She was in the wrong place at the wrong time. But even so, I still want to find whoever did it and kill them myself.

Una's focus is on our hands, and when I glance down, I find myself smiling. "My mother bought me that ring," I tell her. "She said that when she saw it, she thought it was very Shane." My smile widens as I gaze up to see Una smiling at me. "I've never taken it off. I never will."

Una's head lowers, and my body stills as her lips graze the band on my thumb. Her lips make contact my flesh, and I wait for her to sit back up. "I wish I had met her," she says, but my mind is reeling from the kiss to my thumb.

"She would have loved you." I'm searching her face, knowing I speak the truth.

"Sorry, I was just…" Darragh's voice breaks through my thoughts. "I thought you were on your own." He's entered the room, but he pauses and goes to leave and then turns back around.

I release Una's hand, and she stands quickly like we've been caught doing something wrong.

"I better get back to work," she says, not meeting my eye. She squeezes Darragh's shoulder as she leaves. It's a simple touch, but I don't like her touching anyone else.

"You have my attention," I tell Darragh. He hesitates at the door. "You're wasting my time, Darragh. Come in." Even looking at him makes me want to hurt him.

"It's okay," he tells me, turning back toward the door.

"Close the door and sit down." I push the mug and plate away from me as Darragh closes the door. I don't need any temptations. I even move my chair away from the table and pull up one of my legs onto the other to create some kind of barrier.

"I'm having a—"

I cut him off as he goes to sit on Una's chair. "Don't sit there."

"Where would you like me to sit?" He shakes his head as he speaks, and I point at the chair opposite me. He sits down with a huff.

"You kill people, and you don't seem to care," he says, anger lacing every word.

"Is that a question?" I ask. I'm not sure what he's doing here.

"No." He grits his teeth and shifts on the chair. "I can't sleep."

I release my leg. I'm done with this conversation. "Go to a doctor."

"I can't sleep because I keep seeing her face." He swallows, and his brows pull down.

"Whose face? What have you done?" I sit forward, questioning what kind of mess I have to clean up now.

"Siobhan's aunt. I keep seeing her face. It doesn't seem to matter how much drink I consume. She's still there. Her head is all smashed in. Blood bubbles from her mouth."

The sad part is, I understand how he feels. I have to live with the nine lives I took or helped take. At night, they come for me. Darragh rubs his neck. It's now that I notice the strain on his face, the bloodshot eyes from lack of sleep. He's thinner than before.

"You need to find your peace with her."

His head snaps up. "How?" The way he asks is like I have some secret ingredient that will make all this go away. But it's not that simple. I think about what I do to survive. If it becomes a question of me or them, it's an easy one to pick.

"Think about why you killed her. You need to remind yourself that she attacked." I wanted to say it was a life-or-death situation, but with Darragh, I didn't think it was. I was pretty sure he lost control.

"She didn't attack me." The confession pours from him quickly. "I wanted to know how it felt. I wanted to be like you and Liam. I wanted…"

I stand up, closing my eyes and cutting him off. I can't believe what I'm hearing. "You wanted to know how taking someone's life felt?" Oh, God. This was much worse than I could have imagined. I always knew it hadn't been self-defense, and that was disturbing enough. But to think he did it so he knew how it felt…

"Yes, and I wanted to be accepted by Dad." He's shouting, and I can't stop the laughter that bubbles from my mouth.

"How did it feel, baby brother? Did you enjoy taking her life?" I ask when the laughter dies down.

"Fuck off," he tells me, getting up to leave.

"You're a coward. I'm ashamed to call you my brother." My words have him pausing, but he rips the door open and storms from the room. I should stay and let him go, but I can't.

"You couldn't even finish her, Darragh," I shout. He pauses, the rise and fall of his shoulders noticeable. "Once again, me and Liam had to clean up your mess. You couldn't even kill an old woman." I was jagging him. I wanted him to face what he had done. He turns with clenched fists.

"Shut up. I'm glad I'm not a killer like you. How many lives have you taken?" He starts walking back to me, screaming at me. "Who tattoos themselves every time they take a life?" He's reached me, and we're toe to toe. "You wear your kills like a fucking badge."

"Darragh." It's Liam. Darragh deflates straight away. He doesn't step away from me, and he's huffing and puffing.

"Darragh. Leave." Liam's raised voice has Darragh stepping away and racing down the hall. Liam takes a few steps toward me. "What has he done?"

"He killed that woman just to kill her." Even as I speak, I'm struggling to accept that he really did it. Taking a life comes down to a final decision—it's either you or them. That's how I always say it. There are no half measures, and in our line of business, people die. But each one has a reason. To have none... I can't imagine it.

"You have to leave this alone, Shane." I snap my gaze up to Liam, and I don't expect him to start shouting, but his easy words have me shaking my head.

"What do you do when he kills someone else, and then the bodies are stacking up?"

"He won't." Liam sounds sure.

"He killed, Liam, just to know how it felt." When Liam looks at me, there's something in him that I don't recognize, and now I ponder if that's what he and Darragh have in common. Does Liam recognize the darkness in Darragh that I see in Liam? I could never tell what it is, but what if it's this?

"Have you ever killed for no reason?" I ask, not backing away from this. I need to know who I'm sleeping under the same roof with.

"No. But I've been curious."

"I've been curious when I heard older men talk about it. I wondered what it would be like. I didn't go out and actually do it. I'm curious about a lot of things, Liam. It doesn't mean I act on them." I can't believe he would try to dismiss this.

"It's our fault that he's like this."

"I feel like you've put two and two together and got fifty," I tell Liam, not accepting what I'm hearing.

"We've always pushed him away, and this is our price." I glance down the hall that Darragh disappeared down.

"We treat Finn worse, and he hasn't killed anyone for the fun of it."

"We don't know that." Liam blinks as Mary makes her way down the hall.

"Leave it with me. Let me deal with it," he asks as we stand shoulder to shoulder, facing each other. I always place my trust in Liam, but I'm not sure I can let this one lie. I nod at Liam, and he nods back before leaving.

I go outside and the smell of fresh air is nice. I still can't shake off what Darragh has done. Flaming red hair comes into view. I need to check on Una. I hate it more now that she hung out with Darragh. What if he gets an impulse again, only this time it's Una he hurts? Something sits on my chest, and I breathe in through my nose and out through my mouth.

"Hi." Una is waving at me while she leans on a pitchfork, and her voice settles me, the weight lifting off my chest.

"Hi," I say and walk toward her while stuffing my hands into my pockets. It gets them out of the cold, but it's also something to do as Una smirks while she studies me.

"Just wanted to check on you," I say when I reach her, and her smirk turns into a full smile.

"Make sure I'm doing my work?" she teases.

"No. I wanted to make sure you were okay after our conversation."

Her smile slips, but her eyes still hold it. "That's really sweet of you."

I give a short laugh. "Sweet? I don't think anyone has ever called me sweet before."

Una is trying to suppress a smile, but she fails. We're smiling at each other when my phone rings.

"Just give me a second," I say as I pull it out of my pocket and see Neill's name on the screen.

"Go ahead," I tell him as I take a few steps away from Una, not wanting her to hear the conversation.

"At a fight last night, one of the guys dropped dead. I knew he was off his head, but I thought it was cocaine or something. It's that new stuff from Bernard, and I managed to get some for you," Neill says proudly, and he should be.

"I'll be around soon to pick it up," I tell him before hanging up. Una is still observing me and wears a smile on her face. "My mind is still reeling with you calling me sweet," I say because I want her to continue to smile.

This time she laughs. "I regret saying it already. I think your ego is big enough, Shane."

"*Tá tú go hálainn,*" I say in Irish. I'm too much of a chicken to say it in English. But I realize my mistake when Una turns red and repeats my words to me in English.

"You think I'm beautiful?" Why does she sound like she doesn't believe me?

"Now I think our egos are the same," I tell her and something crosses her face.

She doesn't focus on me as she speaks. "You said that for my ego."

I can hear the hurt in her words, and I question why everything I say comes across as an insult. I take a step toward her, and she tilts her head up. Her eyes shift left and then to the right. I keep my focus on Una. "I said that because I do think you are very beautiful."

She smiles but covers her mouth with a gloved hand. My heart pounds as I remove the shovel from her hands and place it against the wall. Una's hands fall to her side, but I take up the right one and remove her work glove. I raise her hand to my mouth. Her eyes are wide, and her mouth has formed a small *o* as I place a kiss to the inside of her wrist.

Her pulse beats quickly against my lips, and it satisfies me that I've evoked that emotion in her. I want to linger longer; kissing her flesh is sending waves through my body. But I tell myself not yet. I stand up straight and put her glove back on. She's still focused on me with pure awe on her face, and I want to kiss her lips. I find myself leaning in, and she swallows hard before wetting her lips.

A horse neighs a few stalls down, and Una clears her throat.

"I have to go. I might see you later," I tell her, and she nods. She doesn't smile but watches me leave. I glance back at her, and she's still staring at me, and now I smile.

I wish I didn't have to go. I ring Neill back as I make my way to my car. He answers on the second ring.

"I need a job done. Are you up for it?" I smile when he repeatedly says yes. I remember now why I like him. "I need that stuff sent up to Dublin. I've a friend, Rachel, who works in the Dublin lab. She'll expect you in one hour. Can you do that?"

"Yeah, of course, man. No problem. Consider it done." Neill's answer is quick, but I won't consider anything done until it's done.

"I'll text you the address," I tell him and hang up. I need to see what's in this new drug and if we can replicate it—hopefully cheaper than what Bernard is selling it for.

Once I text him, I get into my car and visit some old friends to see if they've heard anything about Bernard or Connor. But all avenues turn out to be dead ends. No one seems to know anything.

To me, that's worse than someone knowing something. They're being careful, and careful people are dangerous people in my eyes. It means they have something to hide.

I return home to a dark house. It's two in the morning when I get inside and make my way to Una's room. She's asleep, and I can't stop the smile when I see she's wearing my T-shirt. I don't stay long tonight. Instead, I go to my room and take a quick shower before getting into bed.

I get up around nine and get dressed. Pushing open Una's door, I'm surprised to see her bed made and her window open. Mary comes out of the bathroom, and surprise lights up her face.

"Shane." She says my name like she expects an explanation.

"Mary," I say back, and she quickly looks away.

"Are you looking for Una?" Her question is said as she polishes the windowsills.

"Why, is this Una's room?"

She narrows her eyes at me over her shoulder. "Yes."

"Since you're keeping records of Una's whereabouts, where is she?" I can see the further annoyance in her eyes, but she shields them, letting her lids close. When she opens her eyes again, she's better composed.

"She's at work, Master Shane."

I'm done talking to her; I leave and make my way downstairs. The smell of freshly baked scones in the kitchen makes me pause, but I don't linger. Instead, I grab my wellies and jacket and go in search of Una.

I don't have to search very hard. She's in the yard with Stephen. I dare him to look at me funny. Today, he decides to ignore me, and that suits me fine.

"I got quite the shock when your room was empty this

morning," I tell her, and she looks up from brushing one of the horses. It's cold this morning, and the tip of her nose is red. Our breaths come out in small white puffs, but Una is alive. The outdoors really suits her.

"You know, I'm thinking of getting a lock put on my door," she tells me, but her words are soft.

I lean across the stall door. "Why? You already have a perfectly working lock on your door," I tell her.

"Yeah, but it's funny there isn't a key? I can't find it anywhere." That's because I took it. But I don't tell her that.

"That is funny," I say, and she smirks.

"So why are you looking for me this morning?" She rubs the horse while she speaks. I'm not even sure she knows what she's doing.

"I was thinking after dinner, we could take a look at that bike of yours?"

She stops rubbing the horse. "Yeah. Yeah, that would be great." She's smiling, and I love that I put it on her face.

"It's a date," I say, and a laugh falls from her lips as she quirks an eyebrow.

"A date?" she questions.

"You know what I mean. I'll mark it in my diary," I tell her with a serious tone.

"Nope, that's not what you said. You said a date." She's unsure if I'm joking or not. "Oh…" she says suddenly. She lets out a heavy breath. "I'd need you to help me get it."

She sounds miserable, and I'm not sure why. "It's at my parents' house," she volunteers, and now I get it.

"I'll be there with you." I hope my words comfort her as she focuses on the horse and then the ground before looking back at me. She's chewing her lip. I don't push and wait for her answer.

CHAPTER TWELVE

UNA

I agreed to let Shane come with me. I've braided my hair to the side. My eyes rise in the mirror, and I hate what I see. Pulling out the restricting neckline of the black polo jumper doesn't help. I appear professional—presentable, as my mother would put it.

I'm wearing black trousers and a pair of small-heeled boots. I'm ready to walk into an office. After grabbing my long black coat, I go downstairs to find Shane in the kitchen. The moment I enter, he raises both eyebrows.

"You look…" he starts, but I roll my eyes.

"Stuck up? Stiff?" I could think of a few more names.

"Older," Shane offers.

"Oh," I say as he stands up and stuffs his phone into his pocket. After getting into his car, I put on my seat belt and open the glove compartment to have a look. Shane glances at me but doesn't say anything. Instead, he backs out of the garage as I continue to have a nosy.

He has chewing gum, tissues, and a pack of wipes in his glove compartment. The middle pocket holds two phones. I glance at him, and he's focused on driving out into the courtyard. There's nothing really in his car, but it's only a few months old.

I wait as he gets out and has Stephen help him attach an Ivor Williams trailer to the back of the Audi. Placing my hand on my leg, I stop it from jumping. When Shane gets back in, I don't look at him but stare out the window.

"You should know you're not walking into a friendly environment," I quickly tell him, already thinking of how wrong this could go. Shane shifts gears.

"I'm used to hostile environments."

I know he is, but still. "My mother can have a wicked tongue." I look at him.

He glances at me with a smirk. "I remember."

I laugh at that. Of course he remembers. How could he forget my mother? "I don't know why she disliked you so much," I say more to myself.

"Most women dislike me." He sounds sure.

"I don't," I say honestly. His gaze flickers to mine, and I hold his stare until he looks back at the road.

"I knew you fancied me," he says, and I laugh—like proper laugh—and it's nice.

"You don't fancy me?" he questions while trying to appear wounded, but he isn't, and I know this is my chance.

"I told you before that I did."

His eyes dart from the road to me. "I wasn't sure if that was the drink."

"It was all me," I tell him. My heart is pounding.

He nods his head. "That's good to know," he says, and I smile at the window.

My smile is short lived as we arrive at my house. My mother's red car is parked in the driveway, and all my hopes of her not being home are dashed. Shane hasn't even turned off the engine when she's out the door, and I can see in her eyes that she's livid.

My mother is still attractive in her late fifties. High cheekbones and full lips are still her best features. Her hazel eyes also show her emotions easily, and I know I'm in a lot of trouble.

"Stay in the car," I quickly tell Shane as I jump out. My mother stares at Shane before her head snaps to me.

"How could you? Do you know how worried I was?" She folds her arms over her white shirt.

"I needed to get away," I tell her. My voice is small.

Her hands rise in the air, and she shakes her head while jutting out her chin. "Una does what Una wants, be damned everyone else."

"No. I'm just sick of doing what everyone wants," I say.

My mother glares at Shane again before turning back to me. "Get in the house." She's pointing at the front door, then she folds her arms again, and I deflate. Sadness has me stepping closer to her. I don't want to fight, but I want her to see me as I am. I want my mother to see *me*, not an extension of her.

"I'm not staying," I whisper with a pleading in my voice that she ignores. She moves around me and is banging on Shane's window.

He's staring at her. Her banging isn't necessary.

"Mum, what are you doing?" I'm beside her.

"Get in the house, Una," she says again as Shane rolls down the window.

"I don't know what she told you, but you can go on home. My daughter is staying here with me."

My cheeks and neck burn, and anger replaces my sadness as Shane addresses my mother in a tight tone.

"It's up to Una what she wants to do, Niamh. She's a woman now." My mother moves back from the window like he slapped her. Her eyes widen with some realization, and she lets out a bitter laugh.

"A woman? Is that what you have been filling my daughter's head with?"

I am a woman, but I can read between the lines and understand what my mother is implying. Mortified takes on a whole new meaning for me. Before either Shane or me can respond, my mother swings around toward me.

"I pray that you haven't been near Liam. Tell me you haven't." Why does she look stricken?

"Mum, what are you talking about? God, you sound crazy." My anger snaps, and Mum takes a step back.

"I can't stop you, Una. But that family isn't right." She's pointing at Shane, but he doesn't as much as flinch.

"They're good to me," I tell her, pleading again and not wanting us to part on such bad terms. "You belonged to it once. You raised me with them. I don't understand," I tell her, and I have no understanding why my words deflate her.

"You've come to get your stuff." She sounds resigned to that fact, but when I tell her I'm here for my bike, hope blossoms in her eyes.

"I need some space," I tell her, but she shakes her head in disgust.

Folding her arms again, she shrugs. "I'm here when you come to your senses." She doesn't look at me as she walks back into the house.

I undo my hair, letting the curls free; they bounce around my face and shoulders like they rejoice in their freedom. Shane loaded my bike onto the trailer. I'm not sure where we're going, and honestly, I don't care. My mother's coldness is cutting me deeper than I expected.

I glance at Shane, but he grips the steering wheel, his face tight. Yeah, he's pissed. Maybe even at me for having him sit there as my mother scolded him like he's a child. I want to apologize, but I don't. I sit back and stare out the window at all the passing trees.

When Shane pulls up at the biggest store in Monalty, I'm tempted to tell him to leave it, but he has taken time out of his day to help me. I unbuckle my belt.

Shane's hand covers mine, stilling me, and I gaze up at him. "Are you okay?"

I'm looking into soft brown eyes. Flecks of gold seem to move, and I swallow. Am I okay? I'm not sure. "I will be."

I'm still staring into his eyes, and my body moves closer toward his. The heat of his hand on mine is sending warmth up my arm.

It's Shane who breaks away, his eyes snapping forward.

"You better get started," he says, trying to sound happy, but the strain in his voice is the opposite of happy. I'm still looking at him, confused at his change again. I'm beginning to think that Shane O'Reagan has lost his mind for a minute or is playing games with me.

Either way, it won't end well for me. I climb out and close the door with more force than necessary. I don't turn to check if he follows. Instead, I walk right into the store. The bell behind me rings, and I know Shane is in. He's beside me in a second.

"You want to tell me what's wrong?" he whispers close to my ear, his shoulder brushing mine.

I'm not doing this here. "Why would anything be wrong?" I ask him sweetly.

"Can I help you with anything?" A tall man—he must be over seven feet tall—approaches us. His voice is droll, and his name tag reads John.

"Yes," I say the same time Shane barks, "No." John departs like a sensible human being, but I'm pissed that he listened to Shane and not me.

"There is clearly something wrong," Shane offers through gritted teeth, and I smile sweetly again while blinking several times.

"You are mistaken." I walk off again with no idea where I'm going, and Shane clicks his fingers while calling John over. It's disgusting.

He rhymes off everything I need, and John makes a joke that a new bike would make more sense.

"Una, can I purchase you a new bike?" Shane asks, but he isn't looking at me.

"Of course not," I bite back.

"See," he says to John, as if to say I'm awkward.

"I'll get my parts another time," I tell John and leave the store. I can't do this with Shane. I'm at the car when I realize it's locked. Glaring back at the store changes nothing. I can't see in, but the Audi unlocks with a click. I climb in and wait for Shane. He comes out, and John is behind him with a trolley of all the parts. After loading up the car, Shane gets in, and I'm shaking my head.

"I told you I would get them another time." I was never going to get them all at once.

"We're here now," he says while buckling his belt.

I want to scream. "Why don't you listen to me?" When I narrow my eyes at Shane, I'm surprised to see him smiling. "You're very sexy when you're mad."

My mouth opens and closes like a bloody goldfish. I have no words. Secretly, I'm smiling, but I stare out the window and don't show it to him.

When we arrive home, Shane drops me off at the front door. I don't argue. I want to get out of these clothes. I enter the house and pause on the third step. The sound of laughter and a strange voice has me walking toward the kitchen, where I find Finn and a girl who is fabulous looking.

She has big brown eyes, long hair, and her complexion is something any girl would envy. Mary is smiling, her cheeks red. Darragh winks as I enter—even he looks happy. There's a nervousness with Finn as I walk in, but he seems to relax when he sees I'm alone.

"Una, this is Siobhan," Finn says.

I take Siobhan's outstretched petite hand. Her skin's so freaking soft.

"Hi. I've heard tons about you," I say, and she smiles.

"All good, I hope." She's still smiling. Her teeth are sparkling white, and when she looks back at Finn, who smiles at her, I can see that they love each other.

"Of course all good," Finn says with a hand over his heart. She slaps him playfully.

"It was all good," I agree, sitting down. Darragh is having a bottle of Miller, but he isn't drunk; he's only started.

We chat a while. When I learn that she's a caregiver at the hospital in Cavan, I have a million questions. What's the worst injury she's ever seen? What's it like to see a baby born? Has any patient ever hit on her, and are there any hot doctors? This gets a laugh out of Mary and Siobhan, but not out of Finn.

Darragh stays a while. He doesn't say much, and at times, I think I see guilt or sadness in his eyes. He leaves, but I stay. I like Siobhan. She's easy to chat to. Of course, she asks me about myself, and I tell her I dropped out of college, and right now, I'm not sure what to do.

Shane arrives in the kitchen, and I think that both Finn and I stiffen together, for two completely different reasons. I tell myself to relax, and when I peek up, Shane is staring at me, not hiding the fact that he's doing so. I drop his gaze, and he comes and sits beside me, so close that his thigh is brushing mine.

"Did you meet Siobhan?" I glance at him. Our shoulders brush at the movement, and all of a sudden, I need space.

"No," he tells me, and I narrow my eyes. She's sitting three feet away, surely watching this. When he looks away from me to Siobhan, he's the perfect gentleman and takes her hand in his.

"Pleasure to meet you. Finn has spoken very highly of you," he says, and Finn's mouth opens slightly. I don't like the fact that he's still holding her hand.

"Siobhan's a nurse," I say, and everyone turns to me. Shane releases Siobhan's hand.

"I'm a carer," Siobhan corrects me, and I roll my eyes playfully.

"Potato, patato. You practically do the same," I say, and she grins.

"That is true. Just don't tell the nurses."

We all relax fully, and Shane soon excuses himself. I'm tempted to follow him but don't. The conversation flows easily, and when Finn keeps throwing glances at the door, I question if he's waiting for his dad to meet Siobhan.

I excuse myself, saying I'm going to the bathroom, but instead, I make my way to Michael's study. I hope he's there. It would make Finn's day to have everyone meet Siobhan. I can see the nervousness in him, but he's proud of her and delighted with how well it went with Darragh and Shane.

I reach the study, and Michael and Shane's voices have me pausing. I don't want to walk in with *him* there, but getting Michael is more important to me. I freeze, as the conversation taking place behind the door is hard to process.

"I have Rachel looking into duplicating the drug," Shane says.

"We can't have someone else coming in supplying what we can't," Michael reinforces, and Shane agrees.

"There's a new shipment arriving in the docks on Tuesday. I have Gary picking it up." There's movement, and I'm not sure what's happening.

"It better be cleaner stuff than the last," Michael says sternly.

"It's seventy percent cocaine. After it's mixed, it will be thirty percent, but that's still high."

I'm moving away from the door, and I'm struggling to breathe. They are drug dealers. *Big* drug dealers. As I pass through the hall, I notice that all the paintings, furniture, and even the rugs are too rich for a farmer. I wasn't aware of this before, but now everything is in my face.

I can't go back into that kitchen. I head toward the front door. I need air.

I find my way to the stables as the first drop of rain falls. The sky is low—gray like my mind. It's a jumping jumble of too much. I'm overwhelmed with what I heard. I question if they could have been code words, but I know what I heard. My heart picks up speed when I think of this family with their secrets.

My mother's warning comes to me now, and I ponder if she knows. She can't; she would never have let me leave. But she must have seen the wealth and known it didn't come from farming. I move into the stable that holds my horse and out of the rain that's coming down in sheets.

Shane is a drug dealer. It's hard to picture, but not. Michael is a drug lord. I laugh, hysteria taking over. Darragh and Finn can't be involved—they're nice. Liam? I rub my forehead. My head hurts, and I know I need to get away before I start to really freak out.

When I climb onto my horse bareback, she doesn't protest. Neither does she protest as I direct her out of the stable. I duck my head under the door, and once outside, rain pelts down on top of us. I move her through the yard slowly.

I want to race, but I wait until we're in the open fields. It's not until then that I open her up. Holding her mane, I allow it all to go and focus on riding her. It's freeing, and I'm shaking but smiling a few minutes later. The rain has soaked me, but that doesn't bother me. The lighting that crosses the sky is what I don't like. I'm in the middle of the field, wet, on horseback. There's an old outbuilding near here; I remember it from when I was young. I gallop there quickly as the storm grows closer.

I can't bring the horse into the outbuilding, but she seems to stay close to the stone structure. I'm lucky the roof is still on it, but the two small windows and door are gone. I'm really cold and pace the small space, waiting for the storm to pass. But time seems to tick by slowly, and the storm grows more frantic.

My horse races away at the roar of thunder. I don't chase after her; instead, I stay and wait. The roar of an engine doesn't give me the relief that it should. I'm being rescued. Dry clothes, maybe hot food. My stomach rumbles. But the idea of seeing them has my heart pounding.

I'm peering out the door and can see the land cruiser tear up the ground as Shane drives like a lunatic . He jumps out and runs straight toward me. I question what he's going to do.

CHAPTER THIRTEEN

SHANE

"What is it with you and water?" I ask her while taking off my jacket. She's soaking through, and a shiver has taken over her small frame. There's a strangeness in her eyes that I don't like. As I take a step toward her, she takes one back and holds out a shaky hand.

I recognize the fear. She swallows while frowning at the ground before looking back up at me.

"You told me that what you do is illegal," she says, and I nod.

"Una, you're soaking. We can talk in the Jeep." I take a step toward her again. Her hand collides with my chest, and she shakes her head.

"No, I'm not going anywhere with you." I have no clue what's gotten into her, but she's upset, and I want to take it away.

"I heard you and Michael speaking," she tells me. Her hand flutters away from my chest and falls limply to her side, yet she still stands tall, holding my stare.

"About what?" I ask, knowing what father and I have just spoken of. I can't hold her eye, because I don't want to see that look in it. The one of disgust and fear.

"You know what?" she shouts, her hand slamming into my chest. My eyes snap to her face. My chest tightens, not from the impact of her hand but the way she looks at me. Like I'm a despicable human being.

"Say something." She hits me with both hands. I shift back slightly from the impact.

"What do you want me to say?" I growl. "You want me to paint you a pretty picture? You want me to tell you that you heard wrong?"

She curls her hands into a fist and hits my chest again, and I let her, hoping the disgust will seep out of her with each hit she places to my chest.

"No, goddamn it, Shane. I want you to be honest." She wheels away from me, her back rising and falling quickly.

"Yes, what you heard is true. We make our money by doing illegal… things."

She spins around, a fire in her eyes, and she laughs, but it's full of anger. "You can't even say it," she spits out.

"We supply drugs to most of the Northeast. We earn our money from brothels. We hurt people. We launder money. We're criminals." The more I say, the paler she becomes. But for me, there is something satisfying about telling someone the truth for once in my life.

She stands taller. "Okay. Okay." That's all she says before she walks past me. I turn and watch her climb into the passenger side of the Jeep. I have no clue what that means, but I follow her and get into the vehicle.

Her shivers are worse now. I don't know if it's a mixture of the cold and shock. I turn up the heat.

"Take off your top," I tell her while I pull my own jumper off and fix my T-shirt. When I glance at her, she hasn't moved. "Don't make me take it off you, Una."

She stares at me for a moment before she pulls her top off over her head. I focus my gaze out the window as the rain continues to beat down on us.

The storm is overhead. The lightning is coming quicker. Once she has her top off, I hand her my jumper. She pulls it on, and my shoulders relax a bit more. My eyes move to her trousers, and she shakes her head, but still, she sits up and pulls them down. I drink in her long, creamy legs.

"Stop staring at me," she barks, and I snap my attention forward. I flicker a glance at her as she removes her boots before pulling off her trousers. I don't want to drive back to the house, not with so much hanging between us.

"Did my mother know?" she asks once she has her trousers off and is sitting back up.

"No, of course not," I answer her.

Her lips twist in a snarl. "So, what, you have a secret life?"

To me, it isn't a secret. It's all I've ever known. I can't meet her eyes, not when they hold so much hate.

"What about Finn? Darragh?" Her voice takes on a shriek, the panic rising. I turn to her as she pulls her legs up to her chest. I'm not even sure she's aware of what she's doing. But all my eyes see is her skin, and I pull my focus to her face.

"Yes, it's a family business."

Her mouth opens slightly, and silence fills the Jeep for a moment.

"I'm sorry," I tell her, because I am. I'm sorry that she's seeing this side of us. It's a relief for me but a burden for her.

"Sorry that you didn't tell me, or sorry that you got caught?"

I blink at her. "Both," I tell her honestly.

Her hands are still shaking as she wraps them around her legs. "Jesus, Shane. This is crazy. I just… I know it's true, yet I don't," she says.

When I glance at her, I hate the fear I see. When I reach for her hand, she pulls back, and it's like a slap in the face. I turn to her fully. "I would never hurt you, Una."

She searches my face. For the truth in my words? I'm not sure. But I reach for her again, slower this time, and when I take her hand, she doesn't pull away, and it's like a balm to a burn. The tips of my fingers line up with hers, and I slowly take her hand fully in mine. Once I have twined our fingers, I gaze at her. Her eyes appear huge in her pale face.

"You know that, right? I would never hurt you."

She swallows and then she nods. "I know," she admits. It's a baby step, but it's good.

"I don't want to lose you." When I glance up at her from under my lashes, I can see the rise and fall of her chest. I want her to tell me what she's thinking as a tear falls from her one blue eye.

"You won't."

I smile even though I can still see the uncertainty in her face. She doesn't return it. "Can I take you back to the house to get you dry clothes?" I ask her softly, and she swipes away another falling tear but nods. When she takes her hand from mine, I miss her warmth. I drive slowly back across the fields while ringing Stephen.

"Una's horse got loose. I'm sure I've seen her in the field that runs along the river where the old stonehouse is," I tell him, and he says he will get her once the storm passes. I glance at Una when I'm done with the call, but she still has her knees up to her chest, and her faraway gaze is focused out the window.

Una's in the shower, and I'm sitting on her bed with no idea of what to do. She will have questions, and I'm prepared to answer some of them. I look out again into the hall for the hundredth time, making sure no one is nearby before I close her door over again. This time when I sit down, she comes out of the bathroom.

She's wearing a gray-colored cotton dress with emerald green sleeves and a band of emerald green around the waist. She's beautiful. She pads across the room barefoot while towel-drying her long hair. Her eyes seem to bounce around me, like I'm not here, and I can't sit still. I stand and move toward her. She pauses drying her hair and peers up as I take the towel from her hands and drop it on the floor.

I take both her hands and direct her toward the bed, where I make her sit before sitting beside her. She looks like someone who just woke up, like she's not entirely sure what's going on.

"Are you okay?" I ask, releasing her hands. She immediately folds them across her chest, and I try not to focus on the *V* of the dress where her plump flesh is rising and falling quickly.

"I don't know. I'm just…" She doesn't finish, and when she settles her gaze on me, I glance away. She's hurt. Her lips have tugged down into a frown, and it looks like she might start crying.

"I…" She can't seem to find words, and she stands up, moving away from the bed. When she turns around to face me, my stomach tightens at the intensity of her stare.

"I don't want to get hurt." Her words are whispered, and before I can respond, she does a bizarre thing. Una kneels in front of me and takes one of my hands in hers.

"I know you would never physically hurt me." She speaks to my chest. I'm holding my breath as I stare at the crown of her head. "But it's emotionally that I'm worried about." Now she peers up at me, her eyes wide and softer.

"I will never hurt you in any manner," I tell her while embracing her face. She leans into my hands, and the motion makes me feel powerful.

We stay like that for a few moments before she slowly stands and sits down beside me. Once again, we're silent, but it's a different kind of silence now.

"Do you sell the drugs yourself?" she asks, but straight away, she retracts it. "Don't tell me. I don't think I want to know." She's standing again, her emotions raging. Something crosses her face as she tilts her head. "Does Brian work for you?"

I don't want to lie to her, but she must know that the more knowledge she has, the worse this will be. "Why do you ask?"

"Don't answer my question with a question," she fires back.

"Yes. Now why do you ask?"

She nods at my answer and wrings her hands before she loosens them and shrugs. "Do you try to get people addicted and you charge them, or how does it work?"

I don't like the light she shines on this. "You're a million miles off. I have never touched or sold a drug. I supply. There's a difference."

She snorts, and I clench my fists. "You want to explain to me what this has to do with Brian?" I ask her. Did she see him push drugs on someone to get them hooked? It doesn't make sense.

"Just… it's nothing." She shrugs again, and I'm standing as her eyes shoot around the room, refusing to stop on me.

I stand in front of her, and she has no choice but to look at me. "It's nothing, Shane," she tells me with too much false bravado.

"I'll decide that."

"When I was with him—"

"With him in what way?" I cut her off with a growl.

She throws her hands in the air. "I can't talk to you," she tells me, and I reel in my frustration.

"I'm sorry," I say softly.

She eyes me. I'm ready to lose my cool, but thankfully, she speaks. "Twice, while we were kissing"—I clench my fists but stay still—"he slipped a tablet into my mouth. I was pretty drunk, but I was out of it after that. So whatever he gave me was really strong."

I'm struggling to breathe. A tightness has banded itself around me. Her voice is still there. I hear her words, but it's like she's further away. She takes my silence as permission to go on.

"It was weird. He gave me the creeps, but I don't know. I don't think I'm the only girl he did that to."

"Did he touch you?" I manage to ask, and my voice has her standing a little straighter, like she was confessing to the room, and now she remembers I'm standing in it.

"No. No…" Her brows draw closer as she bores holes into the floor with her gaze. She takes a slight step back.

My hands clench and unclench as I see the growing doubt on her face. There's a pounding in my ears, and my pulse elevates as I walk away from her.

"Where are you going?" She grabs my arm, the panic in her voice rising.

"I'm going to kill him," I tell her and try to walk away, but she doesn't let me go. She's in front of me, her eyes wild as her fingers run across my clenched jaw.

"No, he didn't touch me."

It doesn't matter. He drugged her, and that, for me, is enough. The desire in me to get to him far outweighs anything now.

I remove her hand from my face and take a step, but she's blocking me. I try to calm the rage in me, promising myself that it's only for a moment.

Taking her face in my hands, I want to remove the worry and strain that tightens her eyes.

"Shane, please leave it alone." Her pleas are said through a trembling lip, and I know if she cries, I won't be able to leave.

Quickly, I pick her up. The action elicits a squeal from her. Dumping her on the bed, I leave her room with an order not to follow me slung over my shoulder.

If she does follow, I don't hear her. All I can hear is the pounding of blood in my ears, and the want for violence courses through my veins.

CHAPTER FOURTEEN

SHANE

Smyth's pub has a few lads hanging out in front, all smoking and huddled together. I'm sitting across from it, ignoring my ringing phone. I don't check to see who's calling. I won't allow myself to picture Una upset. I unload the gun regretfully and stick it in the waistband of my trousers before climbing out of my car.

I enter through the lounge where I hope I'll find Patrick. He takes a quick glance up as I enter and goes to return to his conversation with three other men at a small round table, but he does a double take. His brows rise in surprise.

"It's closing time," I tell him, and he rubs his hands down the front of his yellow T-shirt, but he doesn't hesitate as he makes his way behind the bar. As I leave the lounge area and step into the bar, he rings the bell, alerting the younger and louder crowd that closing time is upon them. The ringing bell elicits groans and curses, but the loudest of them all is Brian.

"Nah, Patrick, this ship is still sailing," he tells him. Patrick turns a bit paler as he looks to me. Brian slowly follows his gaze, and it takes everything in me not to attack him. I wait as the bar slowly empties. Patrick rings the bell more urgently, and soon, it's Brian and one of his friends. I don't so much as glance at or acknowledge them as I walk toward him.

"Shane. What's up, man?" he asks, trying to sound calm, but I delight in the hiccup of fear in his words. I shove him into the booth and slide in beside him, trapping him. It's then that I give his friend a moment of my attention—a tall, thin boy with freckles. His eyes shine with too much drink.

"I'll talk to you later," Brian tells him.

"Sit down," I tell the boy, and his eyes bounce from Brian to Patrick, then back to me before sitting down. I nod at Patrick, and he leaves, taking his dismissal. The pub is silent, and when Brian goes to speak, I snap. My fingers grip his neck, and I smash his face into the table, causing all the glasses to rattle. One falls off and smashes on the ground. His friend makes a move to leave, but I snap my gaze to him, and he stays still.

"Jesus Christ, Shane," Brian cries out. I slam his face into the table again, knocking over a pint on his friend, who has learned fast and sits still. Brian's nose pumps blood all down his white shirt as I yank him back up. His blood feeds my rage.

"What's wrong?" He's crying. His hands move to his broken and smashed nose.

"You drugged Una," I say.

"Who?" His response is unsatisfactory. I slam his face into the table again, then I decide he doesn't need all his teeth. I put a lot of force behind it this time.

Blood is everywhere—his blond hair is growing damp with it.

"You drugged Una," I repeat, and his cries come out in whines.

"Shane, I'll do anything," he starts, and I move to smash his face again, but he starts pleading, pushing against my hand. I release his sweaty neck.

"Get me a cloth," I tell his friend, whose skin has turned an ugly gray. When he stands, I see his trousers are stained with all the drink that spilled, but he gets me a cloth. I use it to clean my hands. Brian continues to cry and plead beside me. But I don't feel satisfied. I take the gun out of the band of my trousers, and he slams his back into the wall.

"Ah, no. Jesus. please, Shane." His hands are trembling and raised.

"Una was with Darragh a few nights, and you where there as well. Did you feed her drugs while she was drunk?" I ask while pointing the gun at his head. I know Una told the truth. I need to hear him say it.

"Yes, and I'm so, so sorry."

I slam the gun into his jaw, and my reward is his teeth on the table. "Did you touch her?" I ask.

The no he gives me is hard to understand, but I make it out. I push the gun against his forehead and ask again.

"No, I swear. I'm begging you. Please…"

"Shut up," I roar while I push the gun harder into his head. His eyes are closed tightly like a fucking coward.

"Open your eyes."

He does straight away.

"Did you touch her?" I ask again, and he cries a pathetic no. He's telling the truth, and that gives me some relief. But I want more from him. I use my fists and the gun to pound his face. He tries to cover it with his arms, but I still make an impact. When blood spits back at my face and neck, I stop.

The minute I do, he slumps onto the table. I'm not sure if he's passed out or not. I stare at his friend for a second, breathing heavily before getting up and leaving the pub.

I'm driving home with red hands covered in so much fucking blood. I take a quick glance in the rearview mirror, questioning whether Brian is dead or alive, but something is pushing me back to the house. Una.

I need her now more than ever. I need to touch her and tell the rage that she's fine and that she's mine. I'm not satisfied with just beating Brian. I wanted to pull the trigger.

When I enter the garage, I don't get out of the car immediately. The harsh lights wake me up, and seeing myself in the mirror has me trying to wipe some blood from my face. All I'm doing is smearing it, so I stop. I need a shower.

I don't meet anyone as I make my way to my room. It's something I'll have to deal with later, but right now, I want to wash the blood from my body. I step into my room and pause as Una's head snaps up. She's been sitting on the end of my bed, her eyes downcast, but now her eyes shoot all over my face as she stands. She's shaking her head, and her chin and lip tremble as she races across the floor.

She's wearing the same dress from earlier. Her hair is now dry, and her beauty is all I see. I close my eyes as her hands flutter to my face. She moves my head to the left and right.

"Where are you hurt?" There's a touch of hysteria in her voice, and when her hands run down my arms, I know I should tell her it's not me, but I'm a bastard for enjoying this moment.

"Shane." She's pulling at my top, and I open my eyes. The tremble in her lip has intensified, so I speak up.

"It's not my blood," I tell her as tears slip from her wide eyes. Her eyes slowly move down me, and she covers her mouth with her hand. It trembles, and I take her by the shoulders. She's shaking her head while looking at me.

"I'm fine," I reassure her. She searches my face and then steps into me, her arms hugging me tightly. She's not asking whose blood is all over me. She seems content to know it's not mine. But I want her right now like I've never wanted anything before. Her smell is everywhere, and the thoughts of anyone hurting her, of Brian putting his hands on her, drives a new need.

"I want you," I tell her, and she slowly releases me and leans out. She doesn't say anything but stares at me, and when I pick her up and carry her to the bed, she doesn't protest. One arm hooks under her cream legs, the other at the back of her head. I can't take my eyes off her. I know I need to claim her, brand her, make her mine. Adrenaline still pumps through my body, and focusing on anything tender is hard.

"I need you." I lay her down, and the rise and fall of her chest is the only movement from her. I kneel on the bed and wait for her to protest, but she doesn't. I move over her, positioning my body on top of hers.

She nods, but her eyes are wide with fear and awe. I don't look away from her as I open my belt and pull down my jeans and boxers; I keep eye contact as I reach under her dress and move her underwear aside. I sit myself at her opening, and when she doesn't object, I enter her.

My hands move to her hair, where I bury them. I thrust inside her again, and Una is perfect around me. She moans quietly, her hands clutching the quilt. She's everything I imagined she would be and more. I grip her hair tighter as I fasten my pace. Una releases the quilts, her hands reaching for my shoulders, pulling me closer to her, but we can't get any closer.

I lay my head against hers and inhale her moans. Each thrust I take makes her more and more mine. The ecstasy that crosses her face has me quickening my pace until I fill her. We are both breathless, and we haven't looked away from each other. A tear slides from her green eye.

CHAPTER FIFTEEN

UNA

My body is trembling from the rush of release and also because Shane is still inside me. His hands are still buried in my hair—his hands that are covered in blood. There's a savagery in his eyes that is dying down now as he continues to breathe deeply.

My own breaths are still fast as I continue to take his perfect face in. The blood that flecks his face makes him appear wild. I should be afraid, but a sort of excitement at seeing him feral courses through me. I slide my thumb across his lips, and it's then that he closes his eyes.

I can't look away from him. I can't believe this is Shane. My mind is overwhelmed with what happened. When he opens his eyes, I move my hands away from him. Butterflies erupt in my stomach with the intensity of his stare.

"Are you okay?" he asks. His eyes flicker over the tears that are leaking from my eyes.

I don't know why I'm crying. There's so much—too much. I nod and swallow. Shane slowly extracts himself from me, and the loss is immediate. He goes to the bathroom, and I don't move. But for the first time, I can breathe. The noise of the tap running reaches my ears, and when Shane reappears still covered in blood, I inhale a quick breath.

He doesn't speak, and his stare has rendered me speechless as he slowly parts my legs and lifts up my dress. The lights are on, and there are no barriers. It's like I'm baring my soul to him. The warm cloth he presses between my legs and cleans me with is enough to almost break me.

The gentle strokes. The awe in his eyes. The thoughtfulness of the gesture. I stay still, and when he's finished, he asks me again if I'm okay.

"Yes," is all I manage.

He's standing at the foot of the bed. "Will you stay with me tonight?"

The question has my heart pounding, and I still can't manage words so I nod, and it's enough for him. He goes back into the bathroom, and this time the shower is turned on.

I pull my legs closed. My hand flutters to my chest, telling my heart to settle down. As I lie there, I question so much, like why I still can't find it in me to ask him whose blood is on him. I have a good idea it's Brian's, but it's not the asking; it's that I don't care as long as it isn't Shane's. What kind of person does that make me?

My thoughts are cut off and shut down as Shane comes out of the bathroom wearing only a towel. I suck in a deep breath. His sculpted chest and wide shoulders are enough to make me want to reach for him, but I show some self-control.

I don't know what to call what we just did, but I have never felt more intimate with someone. And yet now, as I stare at his plump lips, I question what it must be like to kiss him. My stomach flutters. His lip tugs up slightly into a half smile, showing some teeth, and I'm like a drowning sailor. I need to pull myself together. I sit up and pull my knees to my chest.

"Are you okay?" This is the third time he's asked me this. I'm not sure what he sees, but I want to put his mind to rest.

"I am. I'm just…" Emotions lodge in my throat. "I'm fine." When Shane drops the towel, I turn into a twelve-year-old schoolgirl, and I actually cover my eyes. A small quick laugh leaves my lips. It's Shane's soft laughter that has me opening my eyes.

"Una, you're blushing," he teases as he pulls on black jogging pants and moves toward the bed.

I'm on fire, so blushing is a nice way to put it.

"It was just unexpected," I tell him as he climbs onto the bed. My emotions jump again, a giddiness taking over.

"You can't just do that," I add before I laugh, and Shane captures my face, my laughter dying in my throat.

"Thank you for tonight," he tells me, and my stomach hollows out at the words. You thank someone who buys you a drink or someone who holds a fucking door open for you. You don't thank someone who lets you see a part of their soul. My breath catches in my throat, and I try to tell myself to calm down. His lip lifts up.

"You look angry, so I must be saying this all wrong," he says, and my heart slows, my temper calming. I don't speak but allow him to.

He smiles and kisses me on the nose. I savor the pressure of his lips on me and think again what it would be like to have them on my lips.

"You were all I could think about. Your face consumed me. So I'm saying thank you for being mine tonight."

"You're welcome." I want to kiss him, but as I move in toward him, his lips move and I get a kiss on the forehead.

What the fuck?

You kiss your grandmother on the forehead. Or I don't know, old people, even someone dying. I close my eyes. I'm overreacting. I need to calm myself. Shane doesn't seem to be aware of the turmoil that barrels through me as he pulls me down in the bed and spoons me. He pulls the blankets up over us, and I'm still not fully accepting that I'm in his bed, in his arms. But there is a blissfulness that fills me again, and I snuggle closer to him.

He claps his hands, and the lights go out. I start to laugh. "That is the laziest thing I have ever seen. And why don't I have that in my room?" I can't see him in the dark. I clap, and the lights come back on.

His smile is wide. "I can get it installed in your room," he tells me and claps, plunging us into darkness, and like the child that I am, I clap again.

"Will I have to tie your hands together?" The question is asked with a serious face, but there is laughter in his tone.

I clap before he can, and the room goes dark. He pulls me closer against his body, and I let the temptation die away and focus on the sensation of his body against mine. It doesn't take me long to fall asleep.

I wake to someone turning on the lights. "What time is it?" Shane asks as he sits up.

"What have you done?"

I don't sit up at the sound of Liam's voice. It's like it rattles in his throat. It's an odd sound.

"What time is it?" Shane asks again and reaches for the black clock that sits on his bedside table. "It's four in the morning, Liam," he barks and climbs out of bed. I pretend to be asleep. I'm not ready to face this.

"Do you know the mess you've made?" Liam speaks again; he's barely controlling his voice. Not seeing his face, I can picture a snarl.

"We can talk somewhere else." Shane lowers his voice, but the threat in his words is clear.

"You did this for her?" He sounds almost disgusted, and it's odd to hear so much in his voice. I move under the blanket before sitting up. Liam's eyes snap to me, and I regret coming up.

"Father is beyond words," Liam tells Shane, his voice more controlled now that he sees I'm awake. Shane ignores him and pulls on a top before coming back to the bed.

"You need to sleep. I'll be back later." His voice is soft, and I'm not sure how he manages to keep it that way as he speaks to me. Liam is boring holes into his back, and I want to warn him, but he smiles at me. "Go to sleep," he tells me again before turning to Liam.

"I'm not talking here," Shane growls, the contrast between the softness seconds ago to the anger now tells me so much. He cares about me. A lot. When they leave the room, I debate with myself whether to go and search for them, but I don't, knowing that would be stupid.

Yet I toss and turn, clapping the lights on and off. I'm curious— will it break if I keep this up? I do keep it up for a while as my mind keeps conjuring up images easily of Shane covered in blood again. What if Liam hurts him? I fling the covers back but don't get out. Liam would never hurt Shane. I clap, turning the lights off, knowing I need to stay put. But what if they lose their cool?

Clap! Lights are on.

What if Shane hurts Liam? *Clap. Lights off.* For some reason, that doesn't bother me in the slightest. I lie down and count sheep. At some stage, I manage to fall asleep.

The moment I stir, all I smell is Shane. The night comes rushing back—Shane covered in blood, Shane inside me. I open my eyes and glance over at his side. It's cold. He never returned. I sit up and gnaw on my lip. I should search for him, yet I know that will make this worse. Maybe he did come back, and I didn't hear him.

I get out of Shane's bed and slip into my room to shower and change. I don't have a clue what to do. Going to work with the horses seems the safest bet.

Making my way to the kitchen is odd now that I'm aware of how everything in this house is paid for. It all seems strange. My skin stretches with anxiety across my face. Entering the kitchen, my pulse jumps, and I pause briefly. Liam is sitting at the table, a paper in front of him. He doesn't glance up, and I question if slipping from the room would be a good idea.

"Good morning, Una," he says, and his controlled voice and suit give me a cold impression. Before, I thought Liam was odd but cute. Now I don't know. A small shiver snakes its way through me. Now, I see someone dangerous.

"Liam," I say, getting a coffee. Mary isn't here, and that's typical. I put bread in the toaster and wait for it to pop, hoping Liam will be gone by the time I sit down.

No luck. I'm ready to butter my toast when he starts.

"We need to talk."

"Fire away," I tell him with as much cheeriness as I can manage.

"What Shane did was reckless and stupid. You know he did it in your honor." His foreign way of speaking seems sinister. "You implied that you had been drugged and raped."

I can't breathe at his words. Is that what Shane thought? Had I said that? No. But when he asked me if Brian had touched me, I couldn't answer him, because I wasn't one hundred percent sure.

"Words can be very powerful, Una. Even more so when they aren't true."

I'm sitting silently, not sure what to say to Liam. My throat burns at what he is saying. "You think I would have lied?" My lip trembles, and I bite it.

Liam shows no emotion as he speaks, and that hurts more. "Did you?"

The chair legs scraping along the floor is the only noise that fills the kitchen as I get up. I'm disgusted with Liam. He knows me better than that. I lean in, supporting myself with knuckles clenched on the table. "You can go to hell," I tell him.

His eyes burn into my back as I leave the warm kitchen and make my way out in the farmyard. I swallow the lump in my throat and try to focus on walking, but my mind won't allow me to.

Fire burns inside me at the idea that Liam thinks I would make something up. I don't know what happened with Brian. I don't think he raped me, but I never said he did. That fact keeps rotating around in my head.

"Morning, Una." Stephen is carrying two buckets of nuts. He places them on the back of a quad. "I'm going to feed the cows. I'll be back shortly," he tells me, and for Stephen, I force a smile as he gets on the quad and kicks it into gear. I give a wave as he drives off toward the cattle sheds that are close to the bottom of the landline.

I find my horse in her stable. She's getting more and more relaxed around me. "Hi, girl," I tell her as I rub her down. Tears burn my eyes, and I stare up at the beams on the ceiling to try to settle myself down.

"It's not bats, is it?"

My heart trips over itself at the sound of Shane's voice. I don't turn immediately as I try to settle the weakness in my knees. When I do, his smile is all dimples and teeth. My stomach squeezes, and I inhale a deep breath.

"I hope not," I say on an exhale that carries a short laugh. My gaze takes him in, and every part of me tightens. His dark denim jeans fit him snugly, and the green wool jumper he is wearing today gives his brown eyes a softness.

I love him.

When I look at him, I fill up with love. I think I've loved him since I was sixteen. The summer he gave me the horse—the summer I secretly stalked him. I take a step toward his smiling face, and it slowly grows serious.

My throat is still burning. I'm an emotional wreck, but I have this need to give him something back.

"I've decided on a name for my horse," I tell him, and he closes the distance between us. His focus is on my hands as he takes them in his before they flick back up to me, causing my pulse to pound.

I want to tell him about Liam. I want to tell him I love him. I want to tell him I think I've always loved him. I need to explain how afraid I am of the rug being pulled out from under me. But I say none of that.

"Summer. I'm going to call her Summer," I say slowly, my own focus going to his perfect moist lips before flickering back to those brown eyes that smile at me, the corners crinkling.

"It's beautiful. I'm glad you finally named her," he tells me as he raises my hands to his mouth. Butterflies dance and swirl in my stomach as his lips press against my flesh, and it burns everywhere. What would it be like to have those lips on mine?

"You noticed I hadn't?" I ask with a breathiness that has Shane staring down at me.

"I notice everything about you," he tells me, and my knees weaken further.

I search his face. I'm not sure what for, but his words are overwhelming me. I hope he never gets used to me. I hope he never stops looking at me the way he is now.

"Why did you not come back last night?" I ask. Shane releases my hands, and the loss is instant. I observe him as he stuffs his hands into his jeans pockets.

"I'm sorry. I had something to take care of. But I'm here now." His words kind of sound like an apology.

"Yeah, you're here now," I repeat back as a smile crosses my face.

His lips twitch, and he lets out a breath on the word, "So…"

"Do you want to work on your bike today?" he finishes.

The idea of spending more time with Shane is perfect, and I agree.

"I've some other work to take care of but after dinner." He takes a step backward out of the stable, his hands still shoved in his pockets.

"It's a date," I tell him, and both his eyebrows rise, making me laugh.

"A date?" he questions playfully, and I shrug at his words.

"Only if you want it to be a date?" I'm still smiling at him, and when he laughs with his head tilted to the side, it takes everything in me not to run to him and crash my lips against his.

"It's a date, Una *álainn*." Beautiful Una. Hearing it from his lips has my heart pounding. The Irish language makes it more. So much more.

CHAPTER SIXTEEN

O'REAGAN
AN CHLANN

UNA

I work in a blissful daze after Shane leaves. I want to tell my own heart to slow down, that it's moving too fast on this, but I can't.

Dinnertime arrives, and I enter the wet room and peel off my coat and boots. The cream wool jumper is three sizes too big for me, but it's warm. I enter the kitchen to find Michael at the table. The moment I come in, he smiles. It's odd. I see him, I do. But knowing the truth makes it hard to hold his stare.

"Una, you don't belong on a farm," Mary says with a smile as she moves past me holding two steaming plates of food. The smell of roast has my stomach gurgling. After skipping breakfast, I'm not surprised. In my wooly socks, I pad to the table and try not to act nervous with Michael.

"Why not?" I ask Mary as she winks at me.

"You're too pretty. You belong on the front of a romance novel."

I laugh. "I don't know what romance novels you're reading Mary. But this"—I point at myself—"isn't it."

I take in the plate of dinner. Marofat peas, carrots, stuffing, roast spuds, and the roast makes this a mouthwatering dinner.

Mary scoffs before getting two more plates.

"Mary is right. You should think of modeling," Darragh says as he arrives into the kitchen with Finn behind him. Finn sits across from me, and Darragh, beside his dad. Now I'm facing all three. When Mary doesn't come with more plates, I'm relieved that Liam isn't joining us but disappointed that Shane isn't here. There's such a weirdness to be around them now.

I give Darragh a tight smile at his compliment, and he narrows his eyes at me.

"Are you enjoying the work?" This comes from Michael, and I finally meet his eye.

He reminds me of the Godfather. My toes curl in my socks as I push them against the floor, reminding myself that this is Michael. The reminder doesn't exactly help. "Yes. Thank you, for the job." Oh lord, I sound so formal.

Darragh continues to assess me, and even Finn seems confused at my tone.

"Good to hear it," Michael says with a tight smile. Wrinkles appear around his eyes, which are sharp, almost predatory.

I focus on my food, shoveling it into my mouth. Darragh's laughter has me pausing.

"Calm down, Una. No one is going to take it from you. Maybe you want to join the cattle outside."

Heat rises in my cheeks, and my whole face burns. I'm staring at a laughing Darragh, thinking he's part of this criminal world. He always appears so carefree, and I struggle to meet his eye.

"Are you okay?" Finn asks, his baby blue eyes focused on me.

Michael is studying me too, and it's all too much. I quickly excuse myself from the table and race up the stairs and back to my room. I make it the toilet before I empty the small amount of food that I ate. Tears stream down my face as my body rejects the idea of what Shane has confirmed.

I can't find the strength to get up. I sit against the wall as I tell myself that this will pass. But it's a bigger shock than I thought.

"Una."

I would roll my eyes at the intrusion from Darragh, but right now, I don't want to see him. Privacy is really nonexistent in this house. Darragh pushes open my bathroom door with his foot. His permanent grin is on his face as he raises both eyebrows.

"I'm not much for a chin wag, but I think you need to talk," he tells me, sitting down on the tile floor with his back against the wall. My focus goes to the gold band he wears on his pinky finger, a red ruby in the center. It's new and isn't cheap.

"Nice ring," I tell him, and he gives it a quick appreciative glance before flicking his hand like a rapper would.

"Yeah, it's alright," he says with a nod of his head.

"Looks expensive." I pull my knees closer to my chest. The black jodhpurs are allowing the cold of the tiles to pass through them easily.

"A few quid. So are you going to tell me what's wrong?" He nods his head again.

I'm not sure if it's for him or me.

"What's a few quid?" My throat is burning now. Sitting here with him, the sense of betrayal is almost stifling. How many times have we partied together, and yet he never told me about his family's true nature? Now I'm giving him every opportunity to tell me.

"Do you want the ring?" he asks while taking it off. I stand, and he frowns at my actions.

"No, keep your stupid ring." I retrieve mouthwash from the cabinet and rinse the taste of sick from my mouth.

"Are you pregnant?" The easy way Darragh asks has me

glaring at him in the bathroom mirror. He stands, his grin gone. When he's serious, he looks so much like Finn. Both are extremely good-looking, and the saying that looks can be deceiving springs to mind.

I need to get a grip. After refilling my mouth with more wash, I gurgle it before spitting out the mouthwash into the sink as I turn around to Darragh.

"No," I answer, holding on to the sink with my hands as I try to calm my racing heart.

"On the rag?" he questions, folding his arms over his chest.

"I know what you are," I whisper-shout at him, and he drops his hands. A smile starts to grow on his face.

"Ah, is that the movie where the ugly guy is a vampire?"

I stare at Darragh, thinking he must be fucking with me. He can't be that stupid. But the smile on his face has me storming from the bathroom and into my bedroom.

"How much was the ring? How did you pay for it, Darragh?"

I can slowly see the realization of what I'm asking sink in. He's across the room in a second, closing my bedroom door, and now I remember the angry Darragh. The one who smashed the chair.

I back away from him and move toward my bed. I don't stop until my legs hit the frame.

"Say whatever you need to say," he says to my silence. I swallow as I search his face. He isn't angry, but there's a strain visible around his eyes and a tightness in his jaw. "Una, I'm the safest person for you to talk to."

"I know you're a criminal," I say quietly, afraid of what my words will erupt.

He snorts but doesn't laugh. "'Criminal' is a nice way of putting it. But how do you know? Was it Brian? Is that why Shane beat the shit out of him?"

"So you're one too?" I find myself saying as I sit down on

the bed. I knew he was, but seeing the answer clearly on his face makes me question my judgment on so much. How the hell had I not noticed? First and foremost, the wealth, yet no one actually worked.

Darragh sits beside me. "Yeah and no." His answer sounds sad, and I glance at him. I can't see his eyes. He's focused on his ring.

"I'm not like Shane or Liam." He speaks to his fingers. "I'm me." He shrugs. "But yeah, I do what they do." We fall into silence.

"So are you going to tell me who told you?" he asks.

I opt for the easy way out. "No one told me. I figured it out."

Darragh's eyes fill with doubt, and one brow rises in question.

"The wealth, but no one works…" I say, and his doubt melts away before he bumps shoulders with me.

"This has got to be our little secret. You can't tell the others," he tells me. I don't meet Darragh's eyes as I agree, but he isn't satisfied. "Una, I'm serious. They aren't like me. Don't ever say it."

"Why? What would they do?" Shane would never hurt me, but the seriousness on Darragh's face has me curious.

Running his hand through his short hair, he stands. "I don't know."

"Would they hurt me?" I ask on a whim.

"Yes." His answer actually surprises me. I don't know what he sees on my face, but he's beside me again. "No, no, I didn't mean that. Look, you can't tell anyone, okay?"

I can sense his panic, and I nod again.

"I promise," I tell him, and he lets out a shaky breath. "I better get back to work." I stand back up, and Darragh nods several times while rubbing the back of his head.

"Right. Glad we had this chat. Good chat." He's rambling as he leaves my room.

I find myself smiling even as dark as this situation is. That tells me I'm going to be fine.

After Darragh leaves, I brush my teeth and make my way back downstairs. I'm on the first step when Shane is there, stealing my rational thoughts away.

"I was looking for you." His eyes search behind me like he's waiting for someone else to materialize. His brows are drawn together; his fingers tighten around the banister. "Finn said you left the table in a rush."

I move down the steps quickly until I'm on the one above his. This puts us at the same height, and my eyes flicker to his lips before I reach up and touch his drawn brows. He relaxes under my fingers.

"It's a bit weird looking at everyone now," I whisper while focusing on his brow. His hand captures mine, snapping my attention to his eyes. My stomach squeezes.

"It's all new. I know that, but you can talk to me." His words are low, and I find myself moving closer when it's not necessary.

But I want to be closer to him. I close my eyes against all the irrational thoughts that are bouncing around. He's making me lose any sense of myself. His hand still holds mine, and I try to focus on the touch, but I can't. It's Shane's touch, Shane's hand that has my pulse racing.

"Una." My name is whispered, and I open my eyes to stare up at him. "You have nothing to fear." His brows are drawn together as he speaks furiously.

I'm looking at this man, and fear of him isn't possible. I'm afraid of losing myself with him—in him. I'm afraid that he might not feel the same way about me that I feel about him. I'm afraid of the rest of his family. Once upon a time, they were mine, but I didn't know them.

"I know," I find myself saying. A door banging downstairs has Shane returning to normal.

"Are you ready to work on your bike?" The excitement in his voice has my mournful thoughts fleeing.

"Yeah, I would like that."

Shane doesn't move. "First, I want you to eat. You left your dinner behind."

I can't stop the smile that crosses my face. "Finn sure gave you a rundown," I tell him, and one side of his lip lifts slightly, like he's fighting off a smile.

"He was concerned."

"About little old me?" I tease, but my words seem to sober up the mood.

"You're safe with us, Una. We all care for you." His eyes roam my face as he speaks.

I bite my lip, chewing on it as I think of his words. Conflicting thoughts rattle around in my head. On one hand, I always thought they cared for me in some way, but now I'm not sure. Their intentions seem different now that I know what they are. As Shane continues to study me, I tell myself that I need to respond.

"Thanks, Shane," I answer, and from the tightness around his eyes, I gather that it's not what he wanted me to say. I'm not sure what he wanted to hear, though. Maybe that I know I'm safe? But I'm not safe.

"Come on. We'll get you food." As he speaks, he turns around and walks down the stairs, and I follow.

***

When Shane flicks on the lights in the second garage, I roll my eyes, and he actually laughs. The sound scatters my nerves.

The garage would easily hold six cars or more, but right now, the center has a beige tarp, and standing on it is my bike, all the parts laid out around it. I walk toward it with my hands behind my back. "You know, the size of this place is scandalous," I tell him.

Shane still wears a smile and places his hand behind his own back as he walks in the opposite direction as me. Both of us circle the bike, staring at each other. It's like a dance. "It's for our bikes," he says with a shrug.

"I only see mine," I tell him, still moving, still smiling.

"I had the rest cleared out," he answers easily, like emptying the garage for me wasn't anything. The garage is virtually empty except for ten large stainless-steel drawers that line the back wall. I'm assuming that's where all the tools are.

I stop walking and so does Shane. My heart is pounding while I gaze up at him. "So where do we start?" I ask while being careful about how I breathe. I want to inhale quickly as my heart demands more oxygen, but I take slow, controlled breaths. When I look at Shane, I don't think I have any impact on him. He kneels down on his hunkers and stares at the bike. He's relaxed, and when I kneel down on my knees, he glances at me.

"We clean it," he says with a wink that nearly topples me over.

CHAPTER SEVENTEEN

O'REAGAN
AN CHLANN

SHANE

As I get buckets and sponges, I leave Una to check out her bike, which she seems pretty taken with. The cleaning isn't really necessary. It can wait until after, but the simple task with Una is all that matters.

When I return, she's sitting cross-legged on the tarp, chewing her lip, and my heart stills. Her fiery red hair is like a halo, and I think again of what this place will do to her. Since arriving, she's lost weight, and dark circles have grown under her eyes.

She's been strong for all she has found out, but I'm not sure she's strong enough. I don't want her to have to strengthen herself to our way. This is why I never got close to her, why I never touched her, and now I'm terrified that I can't let her go, even if it damages her.

She looks up, and a smile lightens her eyes. She takes in the two buckets and sponges that I carry. Once I set them down, I take two pairs of rubber gloves from my back pocket—one is yellow, and the other is pink. I hold the pink pair out to her, but she shakes her head while biting her lip.

"Nope, I want the yellow," she tells me, taking them from my hands. She's trying not to laugh as she puts on her yellow gloves.

"Put on your gloves, Shane," she tells me as she snaps the rubber band at the wrist before grinning up at me.

"You think I'm afraid of a bit of pink?" I ask her, and she laughs. I want to keep her laughing, so I put on the stupid gloves.

"I need to take a picture." She's still laughing as I kneel down and pass her a bucket and sponge.

I open out my arms. "By all means, snap away," I tell her, and she sticks out her pink tongue at me. I'm transfixed and don't look away from it until she pulls it back into her mouth. My focus is on her moist lips. My heart gives a heavy thump, and I glance away.

After dipping my sponge into the water, I start cleaning the frame. Una does the same. I follow her sponge, hitting it with mine and causing her to laugh and tell me to stay on my own side.

There's something amazing about being this close to someone but having a separation between us. I can see everything clearly, but I can't touch her, and that makes me observe her and take every tiny detail of Una in. The freckles that coat the bridge of her nose. The beauty spot under her left ear. Her lashes rise as she pins me with those eyes. Her beauty undoes me all the time, and I snap out of it when she flicks me with water.

"Oh, it's like that, is it?" I say while wiping my face with my sleeve. I'm quick to act and scoop up a handful of water before soaking her jumper. She jumps back with a squeal.

"No, no," I tell her as she picks up the bucket. I hold my hands out, trying to make her put it down. The cold of the water pulls a screech from me, along with a few curse words. She's upended the full bucket on me.

When I blink water from my eyes, her face is flushed with

excitement. We both move for my bucket, and I get it first. She runs, but I use one arm to grab her around the waist and pull her back.

"Okay, hold on. Hold on. Let's talk about this," she says, straining to see me, and I entertain her pleas, moving her slowly toward the wall.

"Talk," I tell her once I have her back against the wall. I keep one arm close to her waist as I hold the bucket with the other—the bucket that she keeps looking at.

"I have a cold, and if you pour that water over me, I'll get really sick, and it will be your fault." She says it with a quick jerk of her head, like she's stating a fact.

Water is still dripping from my hair, but I don't wipe it from my face. I keep my hands firmly where they are. "Not good enough," I tell her, lifting the bucket, and she holds out her hands, touching my chest.

"If you do that, I will run up to your room in my wet clothes and roll around in your bed."

I snort. "Mary will have more work. This is your last chance," I say with a shrug and lift the bucket a little higher. I love the way her eyes dart from the bucket to me. I'm not going to pour it on her, but seeing her trying to worm her way out of this is fun.

Instead, this time, she leans in closer to me, her hands still on my chest, her focus is on my lips, and my heart beats faster under her hands. Her lashes rise, and there's something different in her eyes.

"I love you." Her lips tug down as she whispers it, like she might cry.

My heart is ready to come out of my chest, and I know she feels it. I'm frozen, unsure of what to do. I jump away from Una with a curse as water pours over our feet; I forgot it was in my hand. When I glance back up, Una isn't facing the door.

I want to tell her that it all starts and ends with her. Seal it with a kiss. My mother's voice comes to me, her stupid saying that, for some reason, really sank in, took hold, and has never left me.

The door opens, and it's like a bubble burst. Liam sizes up the situation. Una stiffens at Liam's arrival, and I don't like it at all.

When he turns back to me, his words carry more weight than normal. "I need to have a word with you." I stare at Una, but she's still focused on the door. "Now," Liam adds, and I grit my teeth at his words.

"Una." When I say her name, she peeks at me.

The hurt that shines is quickly covered up with a smile. "Yeah, go. We can do the bike later."

Like a coward, I nod and leave her. I'm afraid she said it as a joke, but it didn't seem like one. Once we leave the garage, I tell Liam that I'll meet him in the library once I change my clothes.

When I enter the library, Liam stands with his back to me. "Your actions have consequences."

My mind hasn't left Una's words. Her face is there in front of me, her lips tugged down as she tells me she loves me. The longer I'm away from her, the more I question if she was messing with me. The part of me that wants to believe she meant what she said is taking over.

"Are you listening to me, brother?" Liam faces me, one hand in his navy suit trousers pocket. He's talking about Father's source telling him that Brian is out looking for vengeance. I don't want to be here, but I'll do this back and forth with Liam.

"I'm beginning to see the funny side of all this," I tell him, and Liam doesn't so much as shift. "So Father has a source who gives him information." I take a step closer to Liam. "Yet"—I hold up a finger—"Father has never mentioned this source to me, only you."

Liam exhales. "Your point?"

My point… I'm not entirely sure I have one, but I know something is off. Or maybe I'm being paranoid.

"I don't know, but why does he not tell me?" Now I sound jealous.

"Because I'm the next in line. You know this. You know you will be my right-hand man. You are already."

Sometimes I feel like a puppet. I've never really cared; I just care about my family. But Una? She's changing me.

"Either of you see Darragh?" I turn to Finn, who hasn't entered the room. The disdain in his voice drips into his words.

"Did you let him off his leash again?" I bark my anger at him, and Finn steps into the room.

"Actually, I wanted to talk to both of you about that."

Liam moves and steps up beside me like we're a united front. With both of us standing in front of him, Finn shrinks back.

"I'm moving in with Siobhan, so you'll have to hire someone else to babysit him."

"So you no longer want to be part of the family business?" Liam asks, and Finn folds his arms over his white T-shirt.

"I didn't say that…"

"You didn't have to. If you leave this house, you leave this family."

I glance at Liam, questioning when that became a rule, but he holds Finn's steady eye.

"What, you want me to let Siobhan live here with you two?" His smirk is joined with a shake of his head. I have no interest in Siobhan, so I step away and sit down.

"He threatened to kill her." Finn points at me, anger growing around him.

"You're still hampering on about that," I say with as much boredom as I can muster.

"How would you like it if I threatened Una?" Finn asks.

I sit a bit straighter, and Liam takes in my reaction. They're aware of Una and me.

"Make the threat," I demand, standing and trying to clamp

down my temper. He won't, but even the thought has me wanting to reach him.

"You know he wouldn't." It's Liam who speaks, and Finn shrugs as if to say he might. "Also, Shane would never harm Siobhan. You have my word."

Finn glances from me to Liam, but his eyes settle on me. "I want to hear him say it," he says to Liam, but he's staring at me.

"Remember that story Dad told you about him and his brother killing the boy?" I ask. Finn's fists clench, but he nods and says a quick yes.

"He lied to you," I tell him and can see color growing in his cheeks. "When the police came, he told them that it was his brother who killed the boy. His brother, Tom, who spent ten years in prison for it."

"He said the father went down for it. That he was an alcoholic…"

I wave off the fairy tale Dad told Finn. "He told you that so you would always protect your brother."

Liam is staring at me, but I hold Finn's gaze.

"So why are you telling me the truth now?" Finn asks.

I don't blame the suspicion that fills his voice. "Because father lying to you didn't keep you here, so maybe the truth will. Maybe working with us more would make you stay."

Finn walks closer to us and I can see the want there. The want that we can never truly fill.

"But Darragh's safety is important," Liam says. "And you are the closest to him." I glance at him as he touches Finn on his right shoulder. "Also, Shane will give his word that he will never threaten Siobhan again."

"You have my word," I say, knowing if she ever needed to be removed, it would be done, but Finn relaxes at my words.

"What else would I be doing?" he asks, and his blue eyes are shining eagerly. I never thought Finn wanted in. I never really thought about Finn at all, only for him to keep Darragh in check.

"I have a few jobs in mind," Liam answers. "But for now, pick one of the outbuildings on the property. Do it up, and you and Siobhan can live there. You don't have to live in the house."

I've never considered leaving our home, but the thought of all of us on the same property doesn't entice me.

"Yeah. Yeah. Okay." Finn smile is wide, and I can't help the smile that tugs at my lips too.

"What about a drink later to celebrate?" I tell him, and once again, he seems uncertain.

"Okay," he finally says.

"We will speak to you later." Liam's gentle dismissal is a reminder of his place in the family. Finn's eyes dim, but he nods and leaves us alone.

"Well played," Liam says, opening his suit jacket and sitting on the couch across from me.

"I wasn't playing," I tell him. My gaze follows the pattern of gold and red swirls on the large rug under our feet.

"You were. You're that used to it; you were doing it without thinking." Liam's heavy brown eyes take note of my every move and reaction. "You need to repair the damage you did with Brian."

I know I do, and I will. But right now, all I can think about is Una.

"I will." I rise but sit back down as Liam speaks.

"You're too distracted, brother. That will cost you."

"I'll fix it, Liam," I tell him with a warning. I don't regret beating Brian. My only regret is not killing him. I have to fix it for the family's sake.

Liam stands and slowly buttons his suit jacket before pinning me with a stare. "Good," he says, and when he walks away, I find myself smiling. He's like Father.

After checking the garage, stables, and my room, I find Una in hers. She's lying on her bed. She changed her clothes to jeans and my green T-shirt. That pleases me. She glances up at me, and color enters her face.

"I'm sorry about leaving," I tell her, walking around her bed so I can see her face.

She glances up again, but her mouth is buried in her crossed arms as she lies on her belly. "It's fine," she mumbles.

I don't want to sit on her bed. I can sense her upset, so I lean against the wall right across from her. "It's just Liam…"

She gets up on her knees, her eyes alive and on fire. "I said it's fine. I don't really care what you and Liam spoke about." Her lips form a thin straight line.

"You're angry." I state the obvious, and she drops my gaze while shaking her head.

"No, it's not your fault," she says, sliding off the bed and sitting on the edge facing the door, her back to me. I move around to her and can see her shoulders tense as I stand before her. "I know your family business, so it's no big deal. We can do the bike another time."

I kneel down, and when she glances at me, I try to keep my focus on her words and not my desire to have her right now. "I know, but my time with you is just as important," I tell her and she quickly drops my gaze before she returns my stare.

"Okay." She doesn't believe me.

I lean in and put my forehead against hers. "I mean it, Una. You are important to me."

She leans away from me, and I give her some space but stay on my hunkers. "Summer is important to me."

"You're comparing yourself to a horse?" I ask, not liking that.

"Should I?" Her words are loud, and her anger is building to a point that I don't know how to contain.

"I don't know what you want from me?" I'm fucking confused. I'm telling her she's important, but I don't think she knows what that means. Saying anything else has me shrinking like a coward. I stand up and let her cool down. I tell her this, and she starts laughing.

"I told Darragh." She's standing, her anger moving her lips. "He knows that I know about your family. About you all being drug lords."

I can't stop the words that bubble up her throat.

"Do you want to know what he said to me?" she asks, but I clench my fists, not answering her. She doesn't want an answer. "To not tell any of you. That I would get hurt."

"You think I'd hurt you?" I ask through clenched teeth.

"You already have," she shouts, and it's like a slap to my face.

"Is this about what you said in the garage?" I ask and her eyes blur.

"God, I'm not doing this with you." She storms into the bathroom.

"Una, open the door."

"Go away," she screams back, but I can't leave.

"I'm sorry," I tell the door, only to be answered with silence.

"Una, please."

"Please leave me alone." Her whispered words sound tired, and when she says please again, I give in and leave her.

CHAPTER EIGHTEEN

UNA

Tears fall quickly down my face as my heart threatens to come out of my chest. He has no idea how hurt I am. I told him I loved him, and he didn't say it back. I know it's not his fault, but it doesn't stop it from hurting. I need him to leave before I say something I regret. Like begging him to tell me he loves me. *God, no one tells you how much this hurts.*

I hear the door close, and the fact that he actually left hurts even more. I can't stop crying. When did I fall so deep? I knew this would turn out badly. If Liam hadn't arrived, would he have said it? I don't think so. Even coming into my room, I really thought he might, but instead, he acted like I was mad that we didn't finish the stupid bike. I'm half laughing, half crying at how stupid I am. Getting up, I don't meet my eyes in the mirror. If I do, I will understand why he doesn't look at me the way I look at him. He's out of my league.

"You're so stupid, Una," I tell myself and leave the bathroom, taking my phone with me. I have one destination—the bar. After snagging a bottle of Jack Daniels, I make my way out to the pool house. Thankfully, Stephen is finished for the day; I don't bump into anyone in the yard.

As I suspected, the pool house is empty. I don't turn on any lights. Instead, I sit down on the couch that's against the wall and stare out at the pool. I sit until the night settles in, the bottle of JD still tucked under my arm. I want to drink it, but another part of me doesn't. In my other hand, I hold my phone. It's sad; I have no one to ring. Acquaintances, I have in the dozens. Friends—zero. I often think I was born into the wrong era.

I set the phone down and unscrew the cap of the bottle of Jack Daniels. The first sip burns, and I let it dull my pain for a second before the pain returns. It seems worse, if that's even possible. Pulling my legs up to my chest, I take another drink of JD as my phone starts to ring.

I laugh when I see Darragh's name flash across the screen. I turn the phone facedown. I lie back and slowly drink from the bottle. The conversation with me and Shane keeps going around in my head, and no matter what way I view it, I can't seem to find the good in it. I say I love you. He doesn't. When he comes back to me, he tells me I'm important. Not losing my ID is important, or something as equally shitty as that. My phone rings again.

"Why are you being so persistent?" I answer.

"I need your help," Darragh responds.

I sit up and drink from the bottle again, but I roll my eyes at Darragh's words. "With what?" I ask, ready to end this phone call.

"Please, Una."

"Are you crying?" I question, thinking he can't be. But he doesn't sound good.

"Can you come and get me?"

I lie back and take another swallow from the bottle. "Can you not ring someone else?" I ask back. The JD burns a path of fire down my throat. It's nice; it's starting to numb me.

"If I could, I wouldn't be fucking ringing you."

"Keep your knickers on. Fine, give me the address." I laugh at my little joke, and Darragh rattles off the address of where he is. He's in Kells and not far at all.

"Give me twenty minutes," I tell him, and he hangs up without even a thank you. I take a final drink before I pocket my phone and creep out into the dark night. An idea starts to form in my head—a bad idea, but it's making me giddy with excitement.

I make my way into the garage and open the box that holds spare keys for all the cars. I get the Audi unlocked with the second key. Sliding into the driver's side, my heart squeezes. Shane's car purrs when I press the button. The rational part of me says he's going to be pissed, but the reckless side of me thinks it's a bit of justice.

When I start to reverse, the garage door lifts up, and I back out without crashing the car. I floor it as I race up the drive, sending dust and stones against the side of the car. I smirk as I hit the main road. There's a sense of freedom as I keep changing gears. Once I shift into sixth gear, I let out a yell. Yeah, this is fun.

The estate I pull into is run down. Gray two-story houses are lined until I can't see them. They don't end but keep going in some infinite line. There is a good chance if I leave the Audi and go and get Darragh, it won't be here when I get back. Darragh had said number three, and I pull up outside the house. No lights are on, and all the curtains are pulled. Several car tires are sitting on the lawn, which is dead and bleeding out onto the cracked asphalt.

I pull the phone from my pocket, then ring Darragh. He doesn't answer. I peer around the estate. It's quiet around, but still, I don't want to chance losing Shane's car.

"Where are you?" Darragh asks when I ring for the third time.

"Outside. Why wouldn't you answer your phone?"

He doesn't answer me. "I need you to come in."

When I start to protest, the asshole hangs up on me.

"Shit," I say as I turn off the car and get out. Locking it doesn't make me feel any better as I walk up the driveway to the front door. I don't have to knock, as Darragh opens the door and yanks me in.

"Does anyone know you're here?" he asks. "Is that Shane's car?" He spins around on me.

I shrug. "I'm alone. And yeah, it's his car."

He closes the door and scratches his neck. "This was a bad idea."

"Yeah, it was. Why couldn't you come outside?" I say, peering around the hall. It isn't dirty, but the simple beige linoleum on the hall floor has lots of cracks and holes in it. The door to the right of Darragh is pine and light enough that if you punched it, your fist would go through. A small lamp that's shining from under the stairs is the sole light in the hall, but I can still make out the paleness of Darragh's face.

"I've fucked up."

His words have dread dripping down my spine. The alcohol burns out of my system as he pushes open the sitting room door. Three dark, stained couches fill the room. A TV that's showing static lights up the room. The light bounces off the face of the girl in the silver disk dress. Her purple lips and still chest have me frozen in the doorway.

"Oh my God, is she dead?" I ask, not taking my eyes off her.

"Yes, she's dead."

I glance at Darragh. "And you ring me?" I can't for a second understand this. My eyes go back to the dead girl. This isn't like the bathroom with the other girl. This girl is dead, dead. Like really dead. My stomach heaves, and I turn, but nothing comes out.

"If I ring my family, they'll kill me this time." The fear in Darragh's words isn't enough for me to not miss the 'this time.'

"You've rung them about a dead body before?" I ask. "Don't answer that," I say quickly as he sits down beside her. "Oh my God, Darragh. She's dead."

When I shout at him, he gets up. "Calm the fuck down, Una. I need you to stay calm and help me, not fucking lose your shit over a prostitute." I stare at the girl again, and my pity for her increases.

"She's a person," I tell him.

But he doesn't hear me. Instead, he lights a fag. "First time, it's hard, but you're part of the family now, and family comes first." He's rattling off words while staring at the girl.

"First time for what?"

"We need to get rid of her."

I can accept a lot of things, but murder isn't one of them. I take out my phone to ring the Gardaí, but the carpet scrapes against my face as my phone hits the skirting board. I didn't even see Darragh move.

"Who are you ringing?" He sounds calm, but it doesn't match his actions. His hand is on my head, keeping my face pressed into the carpet. A terrified part of me questions if he'll kill me, too.

"No one." I try to peer at him, but he forces my face harder into the floor. "Please, Darragh." I whimper now. I was stupid for coming here. He releases me, and I sit up but don't stand. I don't think my legs could carry me.

Darragh is still on the floor. "They will kill me," he says as he peers at me.

"Who? Shane? Liam? They wouldn't," I tell him, and he starts to laugh.

"You have no idea."

A shiver snakes its way around my spine. "Tell me," I say, but I don't want to know. My brain has short-circuited on the fact that there's a dead body not ten feet from me. My ringing phone has both of us jumping, and I don't go for it. Feralness has entered Darragh eyes, and I'm afraid.

"Darragh, please. Let me ring for help."

His eyes snap to mine. "Are you fucking thick?" he barks, and there's a huge part of me that shrinks back and shrivels up at his words. But the survival instinct kicks in, and I stand.

"What do you want me to do?" I ask, but I can't stop the tremble that's entered my voice and lips.

"We need to find something to wrap her in and then get rid of her."

My phone rings again, and Darragh marches across the room and picks it up. His back is to me. I could make a dash for the door, but he's too close. My eyes dart to the dead girl, and my stomach rises and falls. This isn't happening.

"Fuck!" his roar has me frozen as his eyes snap to me. "Did you ring him?" he asks, marching back to me.

"You need to calm down." I push as much authority into my voice as I can. My phone is being waved around in his hand.

"Did you ring Shane?"

"No, Darragh." The fear and upset is in my words, and Darragh pauses his raving and exhales a breath.

"I'm sorry," he tells me, pulling me into a hug, and every part of my skin crawls. I want him away from me, but I force myself to wrap my arms around him. I hope he can't feel the dampness on his neck as my tears trickle down my face. I squeeze my eyes as his phone starts to ring. When he peers down at it, he pulls his hair, but I'm surprised when he answers.

Vicious

CHAPTER NINETEEN

SHANE

"**D**o you have Shane's car?" Liam asks as I sit back on the couch. My head is pounding. An hour ago, I found my car missing, and also Una and Darragh. It's a bad combination. Liam insisted he would ring Darragh before I jumped to any conclusions.

"Have you seen Una?" I stare at Liam as my heart starts to pick up its pace. I'm checking his features for any change, and when he turns his back on me, he's hiding something. I'm standing now, and when I reach him, the call ends.

"Our brother needs us," Liam says as he turns to me. "He needs us to be calm."

We take Liam's Range Rover. "Are you sure Una isn't there?" I ask him again as I glance out the window. He's withholding something from me.

"I told you, Darragh wasn't very clear. Just said he needed us."

I hate being the passenger. Liam is a careful driver, and I'm trying not to tell him to stop the Jeep so I can drive.

"Our brother needs us," Liam speaks again when I don't.

"That's the problem. He always needs us," I mumble.

"Family comes first." Liam says our family motto with a ferocity I understand.

"If she's here, I'm going to kill him." This time, I stare at Liam, but he doesn't flinch.

"She may have decided to go with him. You don't know the facts."

"She's with him, isn't she?" I clench my fists. I should never have left her. She must have gone drinking with Darragh, and he wouldn't take care of her.

"Family comes first, Shane."

I snap my attention to Liam. "She is family," I tell him, and he glances at me.

"She's not blood," he reminds me.

But she's more than that to me. Fuck, she takes place over Darragh any day.

We pull into a run-down estate, and my car is parked outside the third house. I'm surprised it's still sitting there. My focus goes to the house.

"I'll go in first." Liam speaks as he pulls up behind my car. I jump out but wait for him to go first. Darragh opens the door, and Liam steps through. He goes to close it, but I push it open. There's a change in his face—he pales. He wasn't expecting me.

Liam enters a room, and Darragh skips ahead of him. I tell my heart to slow down as a horrible thought comes to me. What if he hurt Una? I step into the room as Liam speaks. "Everyone needs to remain calm," he says, but my sole focus is sitting on the couch.

My heart gives a heavy thud as I skim over the dead girl and take in Una. She's sitting on the couch with tears streaming down her face. She's staring at her hands, which are folded in her lap. Her face is obscured from her hair. I can't take my eyes off her. I can't breathe. Air gushes from my nose.

"Shane, calm down." Liam speaks again. Una's head snaps up, her lip trembles, and all I can do is uncurl my fist and stretch out my hand for her to take. She steals a glance at Darragh and Liam but stands quickly, ducking her head as she comes to me.

Pulling her into my side, I glance up at Liam. I can't speak. If I do, I'll kill Darragh. I'm not sure what Liam sees on my face, but he turns to Darragh. The contact isn't enough for me, but the slap has Una tightening herself closer to me. I wrap my hand more securely around her frame.

"Out of all the stupid and reckless things you have done, this is the worst." Darragh holds his face. His coloring darkens to a gray. Liam has never put his hands on any of us, so this tells me he's angry.

"I didn't mean for her to die." Another slap is delivered to Darragh's face, cutting off his words.

"I'm talking about Una. You had no right involving her in this." Liam's raised words are feeding into the need to hurt Darragh myself, but I'm unable to move. I can't let Una see that side of me, and I can't let her go right now.

"I knew if I rang you, Liam, that you'd kill me." Darragh throws his hands in the air, a shiver in his tone. He's avoiding eye contact with me.

"It's not me you should be worried about," Liam informs him as he glances at me.

"I know." Darragh still doesn't meet my eye, but I can't stand here any longer and not kill him.

I turn and take Una with me out of the sitting room and enter a clean but scarcely furnished kitchen. A large table takes up most the room, and I pull out one of two chairs that remain tucked under it. Once I have her seated, I kneel down in front of her.

"I'm sorry." She swallows her tears as she speaks. My fingers cup her chin and gently tilt her head up. She meets my eyes.

"You have nothing to be sorry for," I tell her, holding her face as gently as I can.

"I stole your car." Her lips are in a frown as she speaks, and my thumb strokes her lips gently. They turn up slightly.

"It's only a car," I tell her, and she shakes her head.

"I was stupid to come here, there's a dead girl in there, and I don't think he cares." Her words hitch at the end, and her eyes blur before tears start to fall again. Pulling her into my arms, I hold her, and she shakes with large sobs.

I'm going to fucking kill him.

"I tried to ring the Gardaí, but he wouldn't let me." Her words have me closing my eyes briefly. She sounds stunned that we wouldn't ring the Gardaí. Her innocence is refreshing and also a reminder of what our life will do to her. She sits back and sniffles, her face flushed.

"You'll ring?" she asks, but she's nodding as if to say of course I will. I don't want to lie to her, but I'm also not going for the truth.

"Let's find out what happened first. Okay?" I tell her, and she nods.

"He rang me. I thought it was to pick him up. I didn't think it would be this." She flicks her head in the direction of the door.

"It's okay now," I tell her, brushing back some red curls from her face.

"I'm going to go in and see what's happened. I want you to stay here," I tell her, wanting nothing more than to scoop her up and take her from this place. But she gives me a little nod, and I press my lips to her forehead before I rise.

I enter the sitting room, and Liam takes a step toward me. The girl is in the same position, and Darragh is sitting on the couch smoking.

"It wasn't his fault. She overdosed. He had sex with her, so he was worried about his DNA." Liam is explaining the stupidity that is our brother.

"Shane," Darragh pleads, and I manage to raise one finger.

"Not a word," I tell him, and he gives Liam a final glance before his eyes settle on the floor.

"I'll get him to ring it in and report it," Liam tells me, stuffing a hand in his pocket. Darragh's head snaps up to Liam, but he has the sense not to speak. Liam's handprints are still on Darragh's face, but it's nothing compared to what I want to do to him.

"Darragh, go wait in my Jeep." Liam speaks to Darragh, but he's focused at me. Darragh gets up and gives me as wide a birth as the room will allow.

Once he leaves, Liam opens the top button of his shirt. "I've never asked for anything from you. I beg you, leave him alone. You have my word he will never go near Una again."

It means so much coming from Liam. If this were for anyone else, I would agree. But right now, at this given moment, I can't.

"No," I tell him and leave the room to go get Una. When I walk into the kitchen, her head snaps up to me. She's stopped crying, but the circles under her eyes have grown darker.

"Liam is ringing the police now, so we better go." I've never seen Una appear fragile. When I reach out my hand, she takes it easily and twines our fingers together. Her face is still tense.

I remind myself I'm doing this for her as I speak. "She overdosed. Darragh didn't hurt her. He panicked because he was intimate with her." My words don't come out as soft as I hoped, but when Una glances up at me, I see a spark there, like everything is going to be okay.

"He didn't hurt her," she says like she's waking up from a dream. I squeeze her hand.

"Of course not. He just panicked." I open the passenger door for her and don't glance back at Liam or Darragh. Liam has started the Jeep but hasn't pulled away.

Once Una is safely inside, I move around to the driver's-side door. It's then I peer up to find both of them watching me. Once I climb into the car, I turn on the heat. She's shivering. It's not from the cold, but I'm unsure what to do, so I just start driving.

"God, I'm so, so sorry for everything," she begins. "I acted like such a child earlier." The car has been moving for a few silent minutes. I thought she fell asleep.

"Una, everything is fine. You did nothing wrong," I tell her, and she falls silent again.

My hands hurt by the time I pull into the garage. I unclench my fists from the steering wheel, and once I knock off the car, I turn to Una.

"He scared me," she tells the window. "I tried to leave, but he wouldn't let me. Only for Liam ringing, I don't know what would have happened." Her lips tug downward as she blinks back tears. She doesn't cry, but her gaze becomes more focused on me.

"He's your brother. I'm sorry." She frowns and shakes her head, like she's trying to stop herself from talking. My silence probably isn't helping, but the idea of him not letting her go is killing me. "I'm just tired," she says and reaches for the door handle.

"I wish you didn't have to see that tonight," I manage to say, and she glances back at me over her shoulder, her eyes blinking with exhaustion.

"Me too."

Una changes her clothes, and I wait as she gets organized before she slips into the bed. After tucking the surrounding covers, I trace the darkness under her eyes. "You need to sleep. Everything will be better in the morning," I tell her.

She manages a weak smile. "Liar," she says, but I'm smiling because so is she.

The relief has me almost thinking of getting in beside her. But I don't. I can't.

I kiss her on the forehead and leave on the lamp as I make my way to the library, where I know Liam and Darragh will be.

The door is closed, but I can hear them behind it. Once I enter, they stop talking, and Darragh moves behind Liam. That sets me off.

I charge him, grab him by the shirt, and drag him out.

Liam doesn't move a muscle, but his sharp words cut through the air. "Shane, don't."

I don't pay any attention to his warning.

"Jesus. Please…" Darragh, the coward, covers his face, but I put as much force as possible into the punch. Holding him with my other hand, I don't let him fall. Liam drags me off him after three punches, but I'm only getting started.

"Family comes first." Liam holds me around the chest. His words are spoken harshly and close to my ear. Darragh is lying against the bookcase, his face a bloody mess.

I breath fast with adrenaline. I'm not satisfied, but Liam repeats his words again, and I try to bring some calm back to me.

"Let me go," I tell him, but he doesn't immediately. "Liam, let me go. I won't touch him." He releases me, but I don't release Darragh from my stare. A shaky hand rises, and he wipes blood from his mouth and nose. Liam walks over to him and drops a white handkerchief into his lap. Darragh picks it up and starts wiping at his face.

"Are you done?" Liam asks me, and I flex my fist, my knuckles burning. I don't answer his stupid question.

"Have you wondered why he rang Una?" Liam asks while he glances back at Darragh, who's still trying to clean his face.

"Because he's a spoiled little prick who thinks he can do whatever he wants," I say, but my stomach tightens at the question.

"Someone told her about us."

"Is there something you want to ask me?" I shoot back to Liam.

"Is there something you want to tell us?" Liam sounds righteous.

"Yeah, that he's always high. Maybe he told her and forgot."

"No, I didn't."

I take a threatening step toward Darragh, and he shuts up, but Liam moves closer to me. "Liam won't always be here to protect you, Darragh. You're such a fucking disappointment to us. To Dad."

"Shane, stop." Liam, the peacekeeper, speaks again, but I don't so much as give him a glance. I keep Darragh pinned to the floor with my stare as I speak.

"It's only a matter time before we're pulling you out of a ditch as you rot away like a sheep." My words have him standing, fire in his eyes, and I grin at him.

"Look, I know I fucked up…"

I have to walk away from his pathetic words. But as he keeps speaking, I turn back around. "I never put a hand on her," he says. His words have Liam closing his eyes, but my whole body tenses.

"I never said you did, so why would you say that?" I take a step back toward him.

"I'm just saying. I don't know why you're so angry." He's still dabbing his nose with his little white handkerchief.

"Shut up, Darragh," Liam tells him, and his eyes widen.

"No, it's fine, Liam." I hold up a hand toward Liam to let him know to say silent as I educate my dimwit brother. "You rang an innocent girl who, number one, is a girl. Number two, she has no dealings with our world. And you don't just ring her to pick you up from a junkie's house, but you what, expect her to help you get rid of a body?" I laugh again. "Are you that fucking stupid?"

"I panicked." He's acting like a victim.

I move quickly and slam him against the bookshelf. "You're a self-centered little prick." My hands go to his neck, and I squeeze. He's trying to claw my hands away from his neck. His eyes widen as he stares at me.

"Shane, let him go." Liam is there now, but I don't let go. His words have me squeezing tighter, Darragh's eyes growing wider. Liam grabs my face. "You're going to kill him. Let him go."

His calm words in a moment of chaos have me releasing him. Darragh falls to the floor, gasping and retching for air. But once again, I'm not satisfied. I can no longer stay in the room with them.

CHAPTER TWENTY

O'REAGAN
AN CHLANN

UNA

I wake up with a racing heart. All I see are silver disks that belong to the dress of a dead girl. Tears leave the corners of my eyes, and I blink quickly, wanting them to stop. As I sit up slowly, I'm faced with Shane's back. He's sitting on the bed, his head bowed. I can't see his face.

"Shane?" I whisper, and his head shoots up. The strain on his face disappears, and his eyes grow lighter.

"I didn't mean to wake you," he tells me as he gets up and makes his way around the bed.

"You didn't." I don't tell him what did. "Are you okay?" I ask. Dark circles under his eyes are worrying me. A frown appears on his face as he sits down on the bed.

His eyes roam my face, and my stomach squeezes.

"You're too kind, Una," he says. I'm not sure why, but I don't object as he moves closer and pulls me slowly into his arms. I come out from under the covers and wrap myself around him while inhaling his scent, and it relaxes me. In his arms, I feel safer.

"I keep seeing her face when I close my eyes," I tell him like a confession, and his arms tighten around me. "What happened with her?" I ask him.

"Her family has been notified. She's in good hands now. Poor girl was an addict." Shane doesn't sound like he thinks she's a poor girl. His words are robotic, and I try to see his face, but he holds me closer. "Just let me hold you for a while longer." His request scares me.

Every few seconds, Shane plants a kiss on my head, and I'm sure his hold grows tighter to the point of being almost crushing.

"Shane." When I speak his name, he loosens his hold on me but doesn't release me, and the longer he keeps me in his arms, the bigger my fear grows. It almost seems like a long goodbye.

"When I saw you sitting on that couch…" He stops speaking and releases me, allowing me to sit back.

I'm on my hunkers in front of him. He won't look at me, and I swallow the ball of fear that has lodged itself in my throat.

"You don't belong here. I've been so selfish holding on to you." His eyes hold such conviction, and my heart slams against my ribcage. "If you want to leave, you can." I'm gaping at him and struggling to breathe. He's trying to get rid of me. Telling him I love him seemed to have messed everything up. I want to take it back, but looking at him, it hurts too much to speak.

"Una, don't look at me like that." He reaches for my hand, and I pull it back.

Tears fall quietly. "I've been forward with you." My nose, throat, and eyes burn, and I have to stop speaking before I bawl. "Too forward," I whisper and wish my stupid emotions would stop until I get the words out.

"I can take a step back," I tell him with a shrug. I sound pathetic. The pity in his eyes has heat traveling up my neck. Oh,

God. Has everyone been laughing at the lovesick fool pining after Shane?

"It's not you, Una."

I laugh at his words, but it dies down and ends on an angry sob. I climb off the bed, needing to get away from him.

"This is coming out all wrong. You're picking me up the wrong way." His words are barked at me as he gets up too.

"Tell me, Shane. Do you and Liam laugh about how stupid I am?" I question, and Shane tilts his head with narrowed eyes.

"What has Liam got to do with this?" He takes a step toward me, and I ignore the tightness that enters my stomach.

"He warned me away from you. Did you ask him to do that because you're not man enough?"

Shane's eyes widen, nose flared, and I'm surprised at the frozen stature of his frame. He clenches his fist. I see the red and swollen knuckles. I'm there beside him, taking his damaged hand in mine.

"What happened?" I ask him quietly. He didn't have this before I went to bed. "What did you do?"

His chest rises and falls quickly, and when I put my hand over his thundering heart, wild eyes meet mine. I want to know what the hell is going on inside his head.

"What I had to," he answers through clenched teeth. I'm shaking my head.

"Shane," I start. He tries to move past me, but I race to the door. I don't have a clue what I'm doing, but the violence in his eyes is scaring me. "You hurt Darragh?"

His eyes snap to me. "Move, Una."

"You can't go around hurting people," I tell him and force as much authority as possible into my words.

"They can't go around threatening and terrorizing you," he shouts back, and I jump slightly.

"It wasn't like that. He was concerned for you."

Now Shane is shaking his head. He's in front of me, a head taller as he stares straight ahead. "Move, Una," he tells me again.

He glances at me as I place a hand on his chest. "I'm begging you, for me. Don't leave this room. Not tonight." His eyes roam my face, jaw clenched. He doesn't answer me, but he doesn't ask me to move again either. I'll take it as a small victory.

God, my love for him is affecting my judgment. With anyone else, I would be long gone. I can't figure him out. I tell myself I'm doing it to calm him down, but I can't manage to keep away from him. My hands leave his chest and roam to his shoulders. I want to pull him into a kiss, but something stops me. Slowly, moving him back toward the bed, he lets me. My heart picks up. Every part of my body squeezes at the thought of having him again.

The weight of his stare nearly undoes me, but I keep some form of control as he sits on the bed. Pulling his jumper off, I inhale the scent of him as my eyes devour his flesh. His muscular torso has me squeezing my legs together.

I kneel in front of him and spread his legs. Shane doesn't stop me as I move close to him. When my lips press against his stomach, the muscles flex and tense under each kiss I plant there. I trail kisses up his chest and along his neck; I have never been so taken or consumed with someone before.

Holding his face, staring into the darkest brown eyes ever, I flicker a glance at his lips. He tenses when I move close, so I place the kiss on his shoulder instead. His hands move now and pull off my top. My cream bra is unhooked quickly, and it finds itself on the floor.

I don't cover myself but allow Shane the same access as he gave me. My fingers sink into his hair as he starts a trail of kisses down my neck. My stomach twisting and yearning building inside me, I'm not sure I can hold on. The intensity grows on Shane, too, as I find myself on my back on the bed. His strong hands and damaged knuckles graze my thigh as he pulls off my trousers. His eyes devour me, and I arch my pelvis up.

It seems forever as he removes his trousers and boxers. His erection springs out, and I'm spreading my legs for him as he moves on top of me. Pulling my underwear aside, Shane places his erection at the opening. His focus is back on my face. Biting my lip is the thing that stops me from shouting out that I need him now.

When he enters me, I let out a long moan. His thrusts are slow and deep, but I want it quick. I want all of him in me. Pulling him down closer by the shoulders, I widen my legs even further, and Shane plunges deeper, faster. I close my eyes as each roll of ecstasy courses through my body. The final one ends when Shane slams into me and pauses as he releases before moving out slowly and back in two more times.

After slipping out of me, he moves down until his head rests on my stomach while he still lies between my throbbing legs. We stay like that as we catch our breath. A kiss to my stomach has my heart picking up speed again. Watching Shane now as he hoists himself off me, my stomach twists and dances. It's there, that stupid three-word phrase that I want to tell him. I drop his gaze.

I don't know what to do as he arrives back from the bathroom with a face cloth and cleans me up. I bite hard on the inside of my jaw so I don't cry. How can I let him go? Once he has me cleaned, he goes into the bathroom and turns on the shower. It's then I get up and put on his green T-shirt and a clean pair of underwear before climbing back into the bed.

When Shane climbs in beside me, my breasts swell in his T-shirt with a want to have him again. The need has me almost turning around, but I don't. He's beside me, and the heat of his body sends me into a slumber. I'm nearly asleep when his arm drapes over my stomach, and a kiss is left on my cheek.

I wake. My body tells me I had sex last night. I still throb. Opening my eyes, my stomach sinks. Shane isn't here. While sitting up, I stare at his side and find a small note sitting on his pillow. I'm smiling like a fool as I open it.

The sun is shining, so get dressed. I'm taking you out.

One line has me racing from the bed like a kid on Christmas morning. I jump in the shower and then spend time picking out a nice cream lace summer dress. It's really pretty, and this is the perfect occasion for it. The buttons start at my belly button and go the whole way to my neck. I leave the top two open and grin at myself in the mirror.

My hair is wild today, and no matter how I try to tame it, curls stick out and spring wherever they want. Today is going to be warm—my hair is telling me that. It never behaves in good weather. Oh, well.

After grabbing a pair of green runners, I slip them on. A bit odd with the dress, but I want to be comfortable.

When I enter the kitchen, Mary gives me a smile. "He's waiting out front for you." Her words have my chest swelling, and I can't stop the ridiculous smile that's plastered across my face.

A squeal tears from my throat when I make it outside, and Shane's lips lift, his dimples appearing. I would be consumed by him, but the Cadillac that he stands beside gets most of my attention. But not all.

"Where have you been hiding this beauty?" I run my hand along the leather roof that's rolled back. I can see my reflection in the black Cadillac—my eyes are huge, and I'm still smiling.

"She's new," he tells me, removing his hand from his trousers pockets. The short-sleeved navy T-shirt is allowing me to see his tattoo in the light of day. The thick black bands are such a statement.

"You like her?" he asks, and I snap my attention back to him.

"It's a 1941 Convertible Cadillac. I mean, what's not to like?"

His smile turns into laughter at my enthusiasm. Moving

around to the passenger door, Shane opens it, and I climb in. I don't say anything about the wooden weaved picnic basket in the back seat.

Shane starts the engine, and I close my eyes in bliss as the engine rumbles under us. "Should I give you a moment?" Shane teases, and when I glance at him, I want to tell him how much I love him. How he undoes me every time I set eyes on him.

"No," I answer, and he takes in a deep breath through his nose like he heard my three words on that one answer.

The wind whips my hair around my face. It's not a pretty picture. It's most certainly not like the movies. It's like a sheep slammed into my face, and Shane has been proper laughing for the last few moments as I battle with the red curls.

"I'm cutting it off," I threaten as it settles. Shane knocks off the engine as we pull in at Dun Na Ri Park.

"Don't you dare," he warns.

"You laugh at me again, and I will," I reply. A yelp jumps from my lips as he pulls me close. My heart slams into my chest. When Shane presses his forehead against mine, I'm disappointed, but also, I'm beginning to think this is how he kisses. Like penguins use their noses, Shane uses his forehead. A quick abrupt laugh leaves my lips. I don't answer Shane's raised eyebrow. Instead, I jump out of the Cadillac.

The grass under my feet has recently been cut, the ends of the grass sending small shock waves up my legs. I glance at Shane as he sits on the rug and eats grapes out of the basket. He packed our breakfast, and it's perfect.

With my stomach full and my soul light, yesterday seemed like a distant dream. "I don't know how you're doing that," Shane says, and I lift a leg before slowly lowering my bare feet into the grass. He visibly shivers.

"Come on, try it," I tell him, but he's shaking his head.

"No, grass and sand are two things I don't like touching my skin."

I roll my eyes. Bending at the waist, I pull out a handful of grass.

"Oh, Shane O'Reagan is afraid of a bit of grass." I throw it at him, and one piece manages to float into his mouth, which he spits out, and I laugh. Laughter turns to a yelp as he gets off the grass and chases after me. My destination is a large oak that stands in the middle of the park. My feet leave the ground as Shane grabs me and spins me around. The world halts as he drags me down onto the grass.

I laugh as he pokes my stomach, and when he stops, all I see is the blue sky and brown eyes, and it squeezes my heart. Shane is above me, resting on his tattooed arm, and I don't move. There is such a seriousness in his eyes that I hold still.

"When you first came to our house, I hated you," he says. Not what I was expecting to hear. His confession has me wanting to rise, but he continues speaking. "I hated you because I wanted you. I wanted you like I'd never wanted anything." His brows pull down as he speaks. His focus is on my shoulder. "I didn't want to ruin you," he says and glances at me.

My heart gallops as he reaches out and moves a curl off my cheek. "I know the right thing to do is to convince you to leave…"

I try to sit up, but his free hand on my shoulder stops me. "Not this again," I tell him as my heart thunders in my chest. He's going to tell me to leave again. My heart can't take this.

"Please, let me finish." He closes his eyes on the word please. I try to remain quiet. "The right thing would be to tell you to leave, but I'm too selfish to give you up, Una." Heat rises in my cheeks at his words.

Reaching up, I hold his face, and he leans into me. "I won't leave, anyway. I'm like a bad infection."

He snorts a laugh at my words before turning my hand around and kissing my palm. Electricity zings down my arm and goes straight to my heart. "My mother, she had this funny saying. 'Seal it with a kiss.'" At the mention of a kiss, my heart grows almost frantic in my chest.

"At night, when she tucked us all in, she would tell us how much she loved us. A kiss to the lips was the final part. She said it sealed in her love, and that when we truly love someone, it's so important to seal it with a kiss."

I nearly can't breathe at what he's saying. His eyes flicker to my lips, which I must have wet a million times since he started talking about kissing.

"I'm going to kiss you now," he tells me.

I'm shaking my head. "Wait." My one word is breathless, but I can't stop the panic that races through me.

"What if it's not good?" I ask, my insecurities rising like a tidal wave to the top. "What if I'm too sloppy or too dry?"

"Una," Shane says, but I cut him off.

"There's too much pressure, I don't know if I can live up to such…"

"*Cunas*, Una." The softness and the Irish word for quiet has my words silenced as Shane moves closer to me. A sense of sinking into the grass and going deeper down the rabbit hole has me holding my breath. His breath brushes my lips, and my hands sink into the grass.

"You look terrified," he says, and I blink, wondering why the hell he's talking and why his lips aren't on mine.

Our breaths mingle together, and I flick out my tongue one last time as his lips brush mine. My whole body seems to sigh before a drum beats within my veins, pushing the blood around my body way too quickly. A sense of swaying as Shane parts my lips with his tongue makes this all seem unreal.

His kiss is full but not urgent. It's slow and perfect, and I can't get oxygen into my lungs. Shane's smell, taste, and mouth are taking over every part of me, and I give myself up to him.

CHAPTER TWENTY-ONE

O'REAGAN
AN CHLANN

SHANE

Una under me is as I had imagined. Kissing her is a high I've never felt before. I deepen the kiss, forcing my tongue deeper inside her mouth, and she gives me entry easily. Her hands grip my shoulders as she pulls me closer. I have to pull back. My body is demanding more, but I remember we're in the middle of a park.

"Wow." Una's swollen lips move. I smile down at her.

"Yeah, wow," I repeat, and her lips tug up into a smile that shows me a set of perfect white teeth.

"Can we do it again?" Her wide eyes and eagerness have me giving her a soft kiss on the lips. "Anytime"—I kiss her again—"you want." Another kiss, and this time, she forces her tongue into my mouth, and I pull back again.

"There could be children around," I tell her, and she nods, fixing her dress.

"Yeah, you're right." Color coats her cheeks as I sit up and take her hand, helping her sit up too. Pressing a kiss to her shoulder, I glance up at her from under my lashes, and there is pure awe in her eyes.

"Tell me about your mum?" she asks.

The question surprises me. "She was really great." Great doesn't even cut it. "She was fun." I smile at the memory of her once waking us up at six in the morning. She had spent hours filling water balloons—she must have filled hundreds of them. She took us outside, and we had the biggest water fight ever.

We were all red and marked when we came inside later that morning, but we were all smiling. Even Liam used to smile then. My smile must falter as Una squeezes my shoulder.

"Are you okay? I'm sorry if I pried."

I cover her hand with mine. "I was thinking about how Liam used to smile more when Mum was alive."

"Liam and smiling in one sentence? Never." Her wide eyes and exaggerated surprise have me smiling again. My lips find hers, and my fingers sink into her hair. Her lips are warm and moist and fit perfectly against mine. She was created for me. My heart thuds as I think of what she means to me.

"I don't think I could ever get used to this." She speaks in between kisses.

"Stay with me," I ask, and she leans out.

"Like in your room?" She seems confused.

Holding her face, I swallow before speaking. "No, stay with me forever."

Her chest rises and falls quickly. "Forever is a long time." Her whispered words are accompanied with blurred eyes.

"Not long enough with you." I wipe away a falling tear. Turning her face, she kisses my hand.

"Forever," she says, and my heart swells.

My phone ringing can't be ignored. I kiss Una on the nose before getting up to take the call. It's Neill. I've been waiting on any word from him about the new supplier.

"What news do you have?" I ask after taking a few steps away from Una. Glancing back at her now, she has her hand covering her swollen lips, but I can see the smile in her eyes as she gazes up at me.

"Brian is out of the hospital and meeting with the new supplier today." The little prick. Liam warned me about this happening. Brian had to know that word would get back to me.

"Where?"

"Smyth's in the next hour."

"Thanks, Neill," I say and hang up. Each step toward Una makes guilt churn in my stomach. I hate that I have to cut our first proper date short, but we have forever to make up for it. I sit back down and kiss her on the shoulder again. Her eyes roam my face.

"What's wrong?" she asks as I kiss her on the shoulder.

"I have to go to work," I tell her. "But I'll make it up to you." A spark of desire flares to life in her eyes.

"I can think of a lot of ways that you can make it up to me," she says, and I kiss her softly on the lips.

"Care to share?"

She bites her lip. "I'd rather show you later."

My trousers tighten at her words. "You're killing me," I tell her.

She gets up while wiping grass off the back of her dress. "Good." She winks before strolling back to our picnic basket. She throws a smile over her shoulder, making all her red curls bounce. Everything about Una takes my breath away.

I hadn't told Una that I bought the car for her. I know she won't accept it, but it's in her name. I put the roof up this time but leave the windows down. Watching Una glance around the car while she touches it like it's a pet lets me know I made the right decision buying it.

Once we get home, I switch cars and give Una one final kiss. "I'll try not to be late," I tell her as I climb into the Audi but roll down the window.

"I'll wait for you." She sways like an innocent girl would, but her words and eyes are full of devilment.

I leave before I change my mind. Twenty minutes later, I pull into Kells. It's two in the day. The pub won't be opening for another two hours. I take my handgun out of the glove compartment. After checking to make sure it's loaded, and the safety is on, I push it into the waistband of my trousers.

I knock three times before Michael opens the door. He quickly steps aside before closing the door behind me. "Shane, this is my livelihood. Please don't wreck it." His words have me pausing, and I give him a curt nod that seems to relax him.

I'm not sure what exactly I'm walking into. I go into the lounge, knowing it will be empty, and then jump the counter. I move down the bar and ring the bell as I enter the bar area. Two men sit at a corner table. Both face me, and I force a smile.

"A drink?" I ask. Brian's face is covered in a white cast that covers the top part of his face, showing his eyes.

"A whiskey," a Northern Ireland accent says. I pour out three whiskeys. Bernard gets up from the table and sits at the bar before picking up a whiskey. He holds it up to me. "To family," he says, and I knock my glass against his.

"To family," I repeat.

"You know each other?" Brian speaks now for the first time, getting up, and I slide the glass down to him. He's too slow, and it slides off the end of the bar and smashes on the floor.

"How's your face?" I ask him, and I'm not sure, but I think his eyes narrow. Hard to tell with all the bandages.

"Michael's not impressed with you crossing the line," I tell Bernard as he finishes his drink.

"Michael? That's what you call him now? I call mine Da."

I smirk, but it's stretched across my tense face. "You've no right to be here," I tell him.

"You think your family is better than mine." It's not a question but a statement.

My heart thumps wildly in my chest. "At least my Da isn't a rat."

"You know each other?" Brian parrots again.

"He's my cousin," I say, not looking away from Bernard.

"They were kids, and name-calling isn't very smart of you," I say through gritted teeth.

"What are you going to do, Shane? You touch me, and the RA will be down here tearing this place apart."

I force a laugh before refilling my drink slowly. "Trust me Bernard," I say and take a drink, "you're not important."

His annoyance grows. "I've every right to be here. You treat your men like animals, so I'm taking over."

I finish my drink, tired with this conversation.

"I'm not looking to get employer of the year. But you taking over? Let's see," I say and decide that he's no real threat. Gary in Dublin would never bend to Bernard's terms; he's too cocky. The real problem is Brian. I need to get him on my side. I refill two glasses, and this time, I walk down to Brian and place a drink in front of him.

"Water under the bridge." I hold up my glass, and I one hundred percent expect him to do the same. Relief swims through me as he picks it up and clicks glasses with me.

Bernard is standing now. "You can't do that. We made a deal."

"The deal is off," I tell him, and his face grows red.

"You can't do that."

"I just did."

"Do you know who I am?" His arrogance is pissing me off.

I move back toward him and lean across the bar. "No, Bernard. Do you know who I am?"

"Yeah, I do. You're a whore's son."

I look away before snapping back and slamming my fist into his face. He falls back onto the ground as I hop the bar. Spitting out blood, he laughs as he stands and wipes his mouth.

"You know she was giving my Da head." He chuckles. My head connects with his nose, and he hits the counter before the ground. I'm down on my knees, my fist hitting his face.

"Stop! Shane!" Brian doesn't touch me, but he pulls me back from the edge of darkness that's threatening to consume me. A pool of blood is growing under Bernard's head. His still chest has me sitting back. I hit him a few times, and his head had collided with the counter, obviously harder than I thought.

"He's dead," Brian says as he places his hands on his head and walks away from me before returning.

"Help me get him out back," I say, getting up and pulling Bernard with me. "Just open the door," I tell Brian as he stares at the pool of blood. I take Bernard out back to where the smoking shed is.

"Get me a towel." When he returns, I tell him to keep the towel to Bernard's head to stop more blood from leaking everywhere. After leaning him against the tin structure, I go back into the pub and start to clean up the blood. I don't think about what happened; instead, I just clean. After scrubbing the floor twice with bleach, I gather all the glasses and take them with me.

"Are you still there?" Brian shouts in from the back like a moron.

I take a final look around. It smells funny, but nothing appears out of the ordinary. Going out back, I give Brian the glasses to hold and take the towel and Bernard from him. I need to get my car around back. I'm about to tell Brian when the back door opens.

"Who's been pouring bleach ov—" I don't turn as the girl speaks, but her words are cut off.

"Ava. Yeah, our friend here pissed himself," Brian says. "We're taking him home."

"Is he bleeding?"

This is too risky, letting her see so much. I shift, and Brian must sense my urgency.

"Yeah, he fell over," he continues. "But you better to go inside and do your job." She must be able to see half of Bernard's face, and that's making me nervous. But when the door slams, I glance at Brian.

I leave him with Bernard's body and make my way out the back of the building. The girl is annoying me. She saw Bernard and me. She needs to be eliminated. After getting the car, I drive around back. My eyes scan the area for cameras, but I know there are none. That's why I picked this small pub. There is no surveillance in this area.

Opening the double green doors that have No Parking painted in white across them, I reverse the Audi in as close as I can and pop the trunk. Once I have Bernard, the towel, and the glasses in the boot, I tell Brian to get in. He hesitates but jumps into the front seat. Closing the gates, I pull away from Kells and drive toward home.

"Who was the girl?" I ask Brian, who hasn't spoken a word.

"Shane, she can't be touched."

I glance at him. "What, is she your sister?" She didn't resemble him, but I could tell they knew each other.

"No, it's complicated. But she thought he was drunk. There's no need to go near her." Panic is rising in his voice, so he must be intimate with her.

"She's a loose end," I tell him while making sure I'm keeping within the speed limit. I don't need to attract any unwanted attention.

"Shane, you have my word that she'll never tell a soul." His word means nothing to me. We reach the bog land fifteen minutes later, and I back up my car into the mud.

"It's too risky, Brian," I say, opening the trunk.

"Leave her alone, and you have me, I will never look at anyone again. You will always come first. If I break my word, you can kill her."

I mull over his words. It would be something to have that power over him. "I'll think about it." My words seem to satisfy him as I start to pull the body out of the car. I should have waited until nightfall, but we don't have that luxury.

Brian follows my steps as we make our way carefully across the land. I send him back for the shovels as we start to dig. I don't bury the towel or glasses with him. Once he's covered over, I take a breather.

"I'm going to drop you back at the bar. You make sure Ava saw a very drunk guy." He's nodding like a fucking dog, and I don't like how overeager he is. But if he betrays me, I'll kill her first and make him watch. "Clean the bar—every single place he could have touched. If I go down for this, so do you," I tell him as I start back to the car. "Burn your clothes."

He nods. "Okay, I got it. Don't worry."

Worry is exactly what I'll end up doing.

CHAPTER TWENTY-TWO

O'REAGAN
AN CHLANN

UNA

It's three in the morning when the bedroom door opens, and I question for the hundredth time tonight if this is going to be my life. I don't want to be all "Where were you?" but I'm curious about where the hell he was until three in the morning. I can see his outline as he creeps to the bathroom. Clapping my hands, the room floods with light, blinding me momentarily. Once I open them, I wish I hadn't.

"What the hell?" There's blood on Shane's clothes and arms. My eyes travel to his feet. "Is that mud?" Muck coats the side of his black boots. *Did he trek through a muddy field?*

"It's okay. My car got stuck." His explanation has me folding my arms across my chest. The small silk nightdress doesn't cover much, and right now Shane is taking me in. For once, I won't be distracted.

"Was the car bleeding?"

Hanging his head, Shane takes a deep breath. When he peers

back up at me, he seems more composed. "I don't want to lie to you," he says, pulling his top off, and he's all flesh and muscles.

My eyes roam his body. There isn't a mark on him, and I'm grateful that he isn't hurt.

"Then don't," I tell him as he opens the belt of his trousers. Pulling them off, he turns to me in his boxers, and it's not fair.

"Una, I do things in my line of work that aren't easy to do."

I tighten my arms at his half explanation. "The other person? Are they okay?" I can't look at him now. What would my dad think of me? I know he's hurt people. I've seen the blood, the anger, yet I love him. What kind of person does that make me? There's a lull, and that's what makes me glance at Shane.

"No." It's stupid of me, but I'm shocked. I take a step away from Shane; I need to think. I also need more answers, but I'm not sure I can take them in right now.

"No, as in he's in the hospital? Or not, as in he's…" I can't finish my sentence.

Shane glances away from me. A muscle twitches in his jaw as he debates what to say. I want the truth, but that terrified part of me hopes he lies.

He settles on "I don't know what you want me to say," and my stomach twists.

"I don't know either." I swallow the lump in my throat, but I have my answer. Whoever's blood is on him is dead. As I sit down on the bed, I try to process this.

"I thought it was just drugs?" I ask the stupid question, and I can almost see Shane grin at my naïve question. He runs his hands through his hair before coming to me. His muscles seem to flex and roll as he walks, and I think it's a nicer thing to focus on. Kneeling in front of me, Shane takes my hands in his bloodied one. We both stare at the blood for a moment.

"Una, I know this is difficult for you, but I would never harm someone for no reason." His brown eyes hold mine, and I nod.

"But sometimes, in this job, there are losses."

"I can't bear to think that one day it will be you." I swallow the tidal wave of emotion that wants to consume me. He pulls me closer to him and lays his forehead against mine before kissing me softly on the lips. I melt into his arms and kiss him like its oxygen for my screaming lungs.

"It won't be," Shane tries to reassure me as his hands roam into my hair.

"You can't promise me that," I say, and he holds my stare.

"If you keep dressing like this, I will always come back to you."

I give half a laugh and half a sob at his stupid statement. He can't actually promise me his safety. All I can do is hope and pray that God keeps him safe. As I flicker my gaze to his lips, I stroke his face, my thumb moving back and over his cheek.

I give a quick glance up at Shane. He hasn't taken his eyes off me before I close the distance and kiss him. My tongue gains entry easily into his mouth, and I give him the same access into mine. My skin burns as his hands leave my hair and roam my body. His touch isn't gentle, and the kiss has grown in intensity to an almost frantic rhythm. We break the kiss as Shane yanks my dressing gown over my head. Our lips smash back together as I move further back on the bed.

My hands roam his wide back as a pool forms between my legs. When Shane enters me, he lets out a moan. His thrusts are as frantic as his kisses. It doesn't take long before I release, and Shane follows shortly after. His head is on my chest now as he breathes fast, and I kiss his hair, running my hands through it, fighting for air too.

"I love you," I tell him as my heart thunders in my chest. It's the type of beat that almost hurts as it slams against my chest.

Shane raises his head and removes himself from me. He climbs up to me. He doesn't say anything, but he kisses me, and I can feel the seal.

The next morning, I wake up to an empty bed. Things always seem better in the morning, but honestly, I'm questioning if going to bed alone and waking up alone is something I can get used to. Do I really have a choice? The idea of not having Shane at all causes me to pull my knees up to my stomach. I can accept having a small bit of him rather than none of him. With that thought, I get out of bed and shower and get ready for work.

After putting on my work clothes, I go downstairs and smile when I can smell the pancakes wafting from the kitchen.

"They smell—" My words fall silent.

"Delicious," Liam finishes for me, and I don't smile at him as he cuts up a pancake. Mary isn't here, but I know Liam didn't make the pancakes. A plate is sitting across from him.

"Sit, Una," he tells me, and I reluctantly sit down. The pancakes aren't as enticing now as I glance up at Liam. The hairs stand on my arms as he assesses me.

"How are you?" The question has me narrowing my eyes, but Liam doesn't react to that. Instead, he waits with his knife and fork poised.

"Fine," I answer, and he continues cutting up his pancake in tiny, little pieces that he chews like fifty times before swallowing.

"How was Shane this morning?" he asks, and I try not to let him see how much he bothers me as I place a piece of pancake in my mouth. "I don't know. He wasn't there when I woke up," I bite out.

"I'm worried about him." I'm not sure if Liam is being sincere or not, but this is about Shane.

"Why?"

"Because, Una, he's acting out against anyone who looks at you funny. I fear you've cast a spell over my brother."

I drop my knife and fork at his words. "No one looked at me funny. Darragh wouldn't let me go; that's not a look. And Brian was an asshole. I don't want Shane go around beating anyone up, but don't make it out like I'm whispering lies to him."

Liam continues to chew slowly, not reacting to my words.

"Screw you, Liam," I bark when he doesn't respond. I take half the pancake and jam it into my mouth, unable to press my lips together, but I chew and swallow the lump before washing it down with a glass of OJ that had also been left out on the table for me.

"I wasn't insulting you. I was stating a fact." The want to stick my tongue out at his righteous tone is squashed as he stands.

"That's not a fact, Liam. You know what? I used to think your weirdness was cute. Now I see you for what you are."

He places his knife and fork on the plate. "And what's that?" I'm honestly surprised he asks, and I have no problem delivering my answer.

"An asshole," I tell him, standing too. I leave my plate in the sink before going into the wet room. It's there that I slip into my wellies and take my coat off the hook. Leaving the house, I slide my phone out of my pocket and ring Shane. No answer. I honestly don't know what he has a phone for.

I don't see Stephen around the stables. He could be over at the cattle sheds; I feed and bed all the horses. I leave Summer until last so I can spend some time with her. The noise of a quad has me smiling. Stephen must be back. I close Summer's stable and make my way to the front yard. But it's not Stephen.

Darragh falls off the quad, his face black and blue. As his eyes snap to me, he glowers. I'm not surprised, but it still hurts. He gets off the ground and makes his way to the shed. I know what's in it, and against my better judgment, I follow him in.

"Darragh." I speak his name gently as he removes a gun from the wall. The double barrel is empty. I know because I checked them yesterday.

"Go away, troublemaker." He's not just drunk. I'm pretty sure

Darragh is high too. The way his eyes grow and shrink rapidly tells me it hasn't been that long since he got high.

"You're in no fit state to take a gun." I'm not rushing toward him, as he doesn't have any bullets.

"You sound like your mother—a broken fucking record. That's why my da had to get rid of her just like Shane will get rid of you." I force a smile even as Darragh's words sting. He isn't himself, and Shane did a number on his face. I have to remember that he has a right to be angry with me.

"Okay. I'm not fighting with you, Darragh," I tell him as he starts opening the cabinet close to the gun rack. He rattles the locked doors.

"Give me the key," he says, and I fold my arms across my chest, satisfied that he can't get the bullets.

"Nope. And I'm doing this because I care," I tell him, and he snorts.

"You're trying to control me like everyone else." The gun is making me uncomfortable as Darragh waves it around, and I have to keep reminding myself that it isn't loaded.

Something my father used to say plays around in my head. "The devil puts a bullet in a gun every ten years." Not a clue where the saying came from, but I'm moving every time the gun is pointed in my direction.

"Give me the key now, Una." Once he doesn't have ammunition, not much can go wrong. I leave the shed, as I'm too uncomfortable with him waving it around. The sound of shattering glass causes a shiver to skitter up my back, and I run back inside.

"There's more than one way to get in," Darragh says, taking a handful of bullets and shoving them into his pockets.

"You're being stupid," I tell him, trying to get him to put the bullets back. But that's not happening.

"I'm going to shoot the pheasant who keeps stealing my boots." He's on the quad, the gun in his hand.

"Darragh, seriously…"

My words fall on deaf ears as he kicks the quad into gear and races from the farmyard. "Shit."

"And you let him leave?" The question Liam asks me has me tightening my fists. His back is to me as he checks the cabinet for the missing gun and bullets.

"I couldn't stop him. You're wasting time. I told you the gun he took," I say, but he isn't listening to me. Once he finishes searching, Liam leaves the shed and starts in the direction of Darragh. I'm on his heels.

"Should you not ring Shane?" I ask, and Liam glances at me sideways. He's walking fast, and I have to walk/jog to keep up.

"I assume I wasn't your first choice. So I can also assume you've already rung him and he hasn't answered."

Liam and his know-it-all ways. I don't answer. He's right, I did ring Shane first, but once again, his phone is going straight to voicemail.

"Go back. I don't need you," he says, and I jump over a log that was hidden in the long grass.

"I don't feel comfortable leaving you alone with Darragh," I tell Liam, and it's weird when his lip twitches.

As we approach the tree line, Liam pauses, and it takes a lot of control not to take a step back from him when he levels me with a stare. "I want to make it clear that I've advised you to go back."

I roll my eyes at his words and move past him. Fingers that are long and cold circle my upper arm, and my eyes snap up to their owner.

"I'm not joking, Una. You're responsible for you." I swallow and nod, and Liam releases me. As we enter the forest, I sound like an ogre moving through the debris. I have to keep checking behind me to make sure Liam is still there. He doesn't make a sound. Lucky for us, Darragh is nearby, and he's making plenty of noise.

"Here, here, little pheasant." He's calling it like you might call a dog.

"The gun isn't loaded," I tell Liam as the world shatters. I'm on the ground, covering my head as everything explodes for the second time. My heart pounds in my ears, and when something touches my leg, I scream. I look down to see a black shoe, and my eyes move up the trouser leg until I stare at Liam, who stands over me.

"Are you okay?"

Am I okay? Two rounds were fired. I'm thinking about how they could have hit us. I'm not sure where Darragh was pointing, but my hands are patting my body down, looking for holes. Thankfully, I find none. I can see the amusement in Liam's eyes. I'm about to tell him that I'm glad I amuse him when a third shot is fired. This one is too close to home. Liam throws himself beside me as wood from a nearby tree sprays us.

"Darragh," Liam's raised voice makes me still.

"That little bitch get you?" Darragh asks while repumping the gun. He's lost his mind.

"Stay down," Liam says.

He doesn't have to. I have no intentions of standing up.

"Darragh, I'm going to stand up. So don't shoot me." Liam rises slowly. I can't see his face.

"I'm so sick of being the last one." Darragh's voice carries such a note of despair that as I lie here on the floor of the forest, something inside me twists for him.

Liam ducks again as Darragh fires, and that has my sympathy fleeing. Is he trying to kill Liam?

Liam's eyes clash with mine. "How many bullets did he take?"

My mind races back to the moment in the shed. "I don't know. Four... five, maybe."

Liam rises quickly as Darragh repumps the gun. I'm moving, reaching for Liam's leg to pull him back down. Four rounds have been fired. There could be one more. The tips of my fingers skim Liam's trousers as he charges toward Darragh. The noise of their struggle has me sitting up. Liam has wrestled the gun out of Darragh's hands.

"Did you just shoot at me?" Liam says. Darragh is pinned under Liam, shaking his head, but it's Liam's fury that seems to be multiplying and growing around us. My lungs squeeze.

"I'm the only one who cares." Each word that Liam shouts is like a punch in the stomach. His pain, I don't understand, but it's etched like a name would be into wood.

"I'm the only one." He's breathing heavy, still holding Darragh down, and I stand up now, but I try to make myself as quiet as possible. Tears run out of the side of Darragh's eyes as he battles with the war that rages inside him. I have no idea what passes between them, but seeing Liam lose control is unsettling. As if my thoughts summon him, his head snaps toward me.

CHAPTER TWENTY-THREE

O'REAGAN
AN CHLANN

UNA

"You let him beat me." Darragh recaptures Liam's attention.

"I stopped him." Liam's voice is calm, but he hasn't let Darragh up.

"You stood there." Darragh's words quiver he shouts at Liam.

"What do you think would have happened if I wasn't there? I pulled him off you."

Darragh shakes his head and turns it away from Liam. Now his focus is on me. "Since you arrived, everything has gone to shit."

Liam releases him as he starts at me. My gaze flickers to Liam, wondering what the fuck he's doing as Darragh walks toward me.

"Liam!" I shout his name, and he doesn't even blink. The bastard. I return my focus to Darragh. "That's not true," I tell Darragh, hating how my voice trembles. I turn and start to leave with a thundering heart. I hold my shoulders high, like they might protect me as Darragh follows me.

"Yeah, you fucked everything up for me. With Brian, Shane, and now even Liam."

I spin around, my temper taking over. "No, you did that. That's all on you and your drug habit. I have nothing to do with any of this," I tell him, and there's some part of Darragh that I can sense peeking out at me behind the madness.

"You're like my brother," I tell him trying to restore some sense to this.

"What, like the way Shane is?" His sneer has heat rushing to my face. "You fuck all your brothers?"

My throat burns. Liam stands behind Darragh, not intervening. My temper flares again. "Just the good-looking ones," I tell him as I force a smile.

"Keep away from me." Those are Darragh's departing words as he walks out into the field.

"Gladly," I shout after him.

Liam stands beside me, the gun in his hand, and now it seems more dangerous than it ever has before.

"Burning the candle at both ends will soon leave you without a light."

My attention snaps up to Liam. "What?" I question.

"Go home, Una." Liam steps out into the field, and I stare at him as he departs. I don't think he means *his* home. He wants me to leave. I march across the field, so done with today.

After a shower and pulling bits of twigs out of my hair, I go to the sitting room to try to do something normal like watch TV. The blue suite of furniture is velvet and has been brushed recently. The marks are visible.

I love the smell of this room. It's like lavender mixed with freshly cut wood. The wood smell is coming from the logs that are stacked either side of the fire all the way up the wall. To get to the top of the pile would require a ladder. But that wood is never used. A wicker basket holds the wood for the fire that isn't lit. I could call Mary. I could light it myself, but I don't. Opening a large beige trunk that's behind the couch, I take out a floral throw and take it with me to the couch.

I haven't been in this room since I was a child. I spent so many hours in here with Connor. He was such a movie buff and easy to be around. He was always kind to me. I put on one of his favorites, Rambo. Not one I particularly like, but one that gives me happy memories.

The credits roll, and I end up putting on Taken, another favorite of Connor's. This one, I actually love.

I'm at the part where the hero is on the boat, and I love when his daughter finally sees him. A knock at the door has me pausing the movie. I'm hopeful that when I turn around, it'll be Shane, but no, it's Liam, dressed in a suit and looking perfect again. I turn back around to my movie.

"Una, someone is here to see you."

I glance over my shoulder, and my stomach twists. My mother's here. My eyes snap from her to Liam, and the soft smile she wears worries me.

"What's going on?" I question, standing up. "What are you doing here, Mum?" She walks to me before pulling me into a hug. I stare at Liam over her shoulder.

"I saw the signs but ignored them," she says. I lean out at her words.

"What are you talking about?" I ask as Liam closes the door and moves toward us. "What is going on?" I untangle myself from my mother. I don't like Liam being here. It's making me nervous.

"I told her about your drug problem," he says.

The color drains from my face.

"I'm going to get you help." My mother nods as she reaches for my hand, but I pull it away. I can't stop staring at Liam.

"Don't be mad at Liam, sweetheart. I'm aware that Darragh got you into it."

I'm shaking my head, trying to make sense of this. "I don't have a drug problem." My words fall on deaf ears. I knew they would.

"You did this to get rid of me?" I take a step toward Liam. He puts his hand in his pockets.

"Darragh is on his way to rehab. He's getting the help he needs."

"Darragh is here, after his little episode in the forest?"

"What episode, sweetheart?" my mother asks. Liam is acting like a normal person would to reassure my mother that the drugs have warped my mind. He's convincing. I'm actually pondering if I am losing my mind.

I have to step away from both of them as I try to gather my thoughts. "This is ridiculous. I'm not on drugs. I'm fine," I tell my mother, but when she reaches out her hand to me like I'm a child, I know she is listening to Liam's lies.

"Come home, sweetheart."

"No." I shake my head while folding my arms over my chest. "You need to go home." I hate the hurt that flickers in her blue eyes.

"You need help," she protests, and I throw my hands in the air.

"He's lying to you. I don't have a drug problem."

"So you're telling me you've never taken drugs?"

The lie is on my tongue. I know how the truth will sound. "I have…"

"Oh, dear God." My mother's acting like I'm the addict that Liam is trying to paint me to be.

"Am I that much of a threat to you?" I grin at Liam, but my temper is flaring. "Are you that insecure about me and Shane that, what, you lie to my mother, thinking she will take me home and your problem is solved?" I'm hitting a nerve as Liam remains silent.

"Oh, you're not with that boy."

I rub my forehead. "Mum, not now. I'm not doing this with you," I tell her as I turn and knock off the TV.

"He is no good for you. He's a thug."

I clench my fists. "So was Michael, but you married him," I tell her, and she pulls at her ear—a tic I'm used to seeing when she's uncomfortable. She's here because she's been lied to.

"Mum, I love him, and I'm not leaving him," I tell her gently, hoping she can understand.

Tears brim in her eyes, and I hate seeing how upset she is. "Your father," she starts, and my heart slams against my chest, "would be so ashamed of you."

My nose burns, and my lips tug downward. "Don't bring Dad into this." It's whispered.

"Shane is no good for you. You can do so much better. An accountant or a doctor."

"My brother is as good as any other man." Liam's words annoy me.

"We all know what Shane O'Reagan is."

My stomach twists at the viciousness of her words. "What is he?" I'm looking from her to Liam, and they're having a stare off.

"Not good enough for my daughter." Her words seem final. "Come on," she tells me, and I can't understand why she won't listen.

"I'm not leaving him," I tell her, more firmly this time. Her lips twist into a snarl.

"If you don't come with me now, you can stay here for good."

I stand my ground even as my heart pounds.

"You stupid girl" are my mother's departing words. I'm still standing in the same place after she leaves, and my mind is caught on one thing.

Your father would be ashamed of you. She voiced a fear of mine. My lip trembles, and I bite it. I exhale a deep breath as my vision blurs.

"I know you don't understand, but I love him, Liam." Tears fall as I face him. "I know I should leave—I know that—but I can't leave him." The thought twists my stomach painfully. Tears continue to trickle down my face. Liam doesn't react or say anything. I didn't think he would.

"I hope, one day, you find love too." I leave the room feeling crushed.

Flickering on the lights in the garage, I focus on my bike. I bought this because of my dad's love for bikes. Right now, I want to be as close to him as possible. I want him to tell me that he isn't ashamed of me. Kneeling on the tarp, I run my fingers along the frame of the bike.

It's clean from the last time Shane and I worked on it. I think my dad would have loved Shane, but if he knew what he did, he would have been more afraid for me. I shake my head as the bridge of my nose aches and sit back on my bum; I bury my head in my knees and cry.

I want my dad back, even if it's only for a moment. I want him to hold me and call me his girl like he always did. Dreaming of him used to ease my yearning. Now I hate how his face is fading.

"I miss you," I tell the empty garage. My tears come heavier. I hate this place. I hate everything right now. It all seems unfair. I want to scream or smash something, but I don't do either. I get up and leave the garage. Right now, I need him.

He's the fifth headstone down, under the weeping willow. Wiping some falling leaves off his grave, I sit down. I haven't been here in a while. The white pot that holds dead flowers tells me no one has. I remove the flowers and sit back down, staring at the headstone. At the start, it was nearly a daily journey for me, and I'd tell him all about my day, but these days, it's getting less and less.

"I'm sorry I haven't been around much." I sit on the curb now, my back to the headstone, and stare up at the tree. "Everything is a mess, and I'm worried that it's my fault." A shiver assaults my body.

"I met someone," I tell him with a smile, opting for a happy story. He doesn't need to hear my woes. "His name is Shane. You'd really like him. The man that Mum married after you, it's his son. But that's neither here nor there. Anyway, his brother Liam is being a pain. He wants to get rid of me. Darragh, who's Shane's other brother, is mad at me too. Oh"—I give a little laugh—"so is Mum, no surprise there."

I focus on my fingers, my ramblings not over. "I left my job, got the courage to walk away. I'm working with horses now." I start crying again. I'm not entirely sure why this time. "I named my horse Summer. You would love her. She's real feisty, a bit like me." I snort a laugh again. "I think she's pregnant, but we'll find out soon." Wiping away tears, I stop beating around the bush. I know why I'm here.

"I'm so afraid, Daddy." I snivel a cry. "I don't want you to be disappointed in me." I hiccup and bury my head in my knees as I bleed my soul on my father's grave. He doesn't answer me, but being here and telling him my fears gives me some comfort.

CHAPTER TWENTY-FOUR

O'REAGAN
AN CHLANN

SHANE

The water is silent as I sit on the bank of the lake. I used to come here with Liam and Connor as a child. That was before we found out he was our half brother. Back then, you couldn't separate us. A smile tugs at my lips now as I picture the three skinny kids in white vests jumping into the lake. We were happy until we had to leave and go home.

The walk back was filled with skitting and laughing. Back then, Connor was the comedian. Back then, Liam smiled. Back then, life had more meaning. The clay on my shoes mocks me. The man I have become isn't what I wanted.

I exhale and stare out at the lake, trying to find a peaceful place in my mind. I've always had to be ten steps ahead of everyone else, and it's exhausting. After leaving last night, I dug up Bernard's body and reburied him on land we own near the Loch Leigh Mountains. It isn't far from us, but after digging up Bernard's rancid body and reburying him, I was exhausted, and not just my body but my mind. I couldn't trust Brian with the knowledge of where the body was. That was my only reason for moving it. I know I'll have to move Siobhan's auntie, too, and the girl from the house that Darragh killed.

I think that's what hurt the most. They lied to me. They told me they were ringing the Gardaí. I laugh now at my own stupidity. Since when do we hand over bodies? We bury them.

Rubbing my forehead doesn't ease the ache there. The whole ordeal makes me question what other secrets Darragh and Liam carry. Why Liam protects him continuously. They share something that strengthened that bond, and now they have another secret that they've kept from me. But soon, they will know that I know. Once the body is moved, they'll figure it out.

Standing, I move around the lake. I want to go home to Una, but I also don't. I don't want to see those same questioning eyes from when I came in late. Worry was gnawing at her, and it killed me. If I'm going to keep her, I need her away from the house.

She'll end up too damaged with all of them. Even with me. But I can't let it go. Tomorrow, I have an appointment to view Deerpark Stud Farm, and the idea of owning it is exciting. That's where I will place Una. She will have a home, a job. She will be safe from my family. It's still close to our home, because no matter what, family comes first. That's inside me, and no matter what, I can't let it go. No matter what my brothers do, I will be there to help them. When you bury a body with a person, you're tied to them for life.

Returning to the car, I take my phone out of the glove compartment. I have two missed calls from Una, one from Liam.

My stomach twists as I dial Una's number, and it goes to voice mail. The engine starts as I turn the key. That's another thing I need to do, burn this car, and I actually like it. I ring Una again, and she still doesn't pick up. I don't ring Liam back. I'm too pissed at him right now after lying to me. Instead, I ring Neill. He answers on the first ring.

"Any word?" I ask while leaving the lake.

"All quiet. Brian is back to business as usual."

I nod at Neill's words. I can breathe for the moment. "Anything on Connor?" This is something that shouldn't have taken so long, but it's like he's gone.

"Not a thing, but I'll keep my ear to the ground."

"Thanks," I say before hanging up. When the car settles in the garage, I want to find Una straight away, but I don't want her to see me covered in mud. Showering in my room isn't an option. There's a shower room off the garage that holds fresh clothes in case of emergencies. I make it quick. Once showered and dressed in a fresh pair of jeans and a red T-shirt, I go look for Una. I ring her three more times as I search the house. I get no answer, and my stomach tightens.

The intensity of her stare as she focuses on the bike has me pausing in the doorway. Red curls are piled on top of her head as she sits barefoot on the tarp. An oversized brown jumper and cream leggings make her look a picture. I'm not sure what's she's trying to do, but I could stand here all day watching her. Her eyes grow wide, and a smile shows a set of perfect white teeth.

"Hi." She's beautiful.

"Hi," I say back, stepping into the room. "I've been ringing you," I tell her, waving my phone at her, and she tilts her head.

"Funny, that is. I've been ringing you too."

Sitting down beside her, my fingers find her hand, and I entwine them. "Yeah, I left the phone in the car," I tell her.

Her smile widens as she looks at our hands before her gaze travels up to my eyes. "You showered."

My heart gives a heavy thud as I see that uncertainty in her eyes again. "I did." I look at the bike now as I clench my jaw. I hate this. I hate how she's looking at me.

Her small, pale hand takes my face, making me look at her. "You smell lovely," she says, her eyes lighter as she dips her head toward me and places a soft, precise kiss on my lips.

"I love you, Shane O' Reagan, in every shape and form." Her eyes shine as she tells me this, her hand clutching my face, like it's by sheer force that I will hear what she is saying, and I do.

She's telling me that she knows what I do and that she still loves me regardless.

"This life that I live is dangerous, but I love it. I love my family, and I know I could never walk away."

Una's eyes are wide as she takes in my words. There's such a look of fear on her face that I pause and press my fingers to her cheek. I'm smiling now at a warning that Liam always gave me.

"Liam used to say that love makes a man weak." At the mention of Liam's name, her eyes close slightly, and that makes me smile more. She isn't a fan, but who could blame her?

"Your love makes me stronger," I admit, and her lips form a small *o,* and her chest starts to rise and fall wildly. "You're intoxicating, Una, and I want to share all of this with you. The moments I hold on to the most are the ones with you in them. I love you."

A tear trickles down her face. "Wow," she says through a half sob, half laugh. "Seal with a kiss," she tells me.

My chest tightens, but I don't hesitate. I seal our love with a kiss that reaches inside me and heals some dark part of me that had me keeping Una away. Now she's in fully.

The clearing of a throat is what breaks the kiss. Finn is wearing a goofy smile, and I can't hide my own.

"Dad has surprised us all with a family meal."

I raise my eyebrows, hoping Finn can shed some light on this family meal. Dad doesn't do anything for nothing, but Finn shrugs.

"Siobhan's coming." Finn sounds nervous as he tells Una, who still clutches my hand.

"She's so sweet, Finn. This is going to be fun." Her words have Finn relaxing, and when she rests her head on my shoulder, I can't help but relax even further.

Liam and Dad are the only two in the dining room when Una and I arrive. Liam looks up, and there's something in the way he looks at Una that I don't like.

"Liam," she greets him sharply with a raised chin.

"Una," he responds, but he adds a nod of his head. Like approval or something.

Dad has been looking at my and Una's joined hands, and when I meet his eye, he doesn't show what he feels. Releasing my hand, Una sits down beside Dad, but first kisses him softly on the cheek. His face melts, and a smile is there just for Una. I don't mind. As long as he's kind to her, that's all that matters. I sit beside Una and across from Liam, who stares at me.

"Hi." A shy voice at the dining room door has us all looking to Siobhan.

Una gives a seriously enthusiastic wave beside me, and I can't stop smiling. Siobhan slides in beside Liam without hesitation, and sitting opposite him, seeing him sitting beside a girl, is almost amusing. Has he ever pictured himself settling down? He was too used to the whores he managed.

"Siobhan, I'm glad you could come." Dad sounds like he means it, but I'm still nervous about why we're all gathered around this time. It's like the last supper. Finn nods at everyone, hands jammed into his pockets, before he sits down beside Siobhan.

"Thank you so much for the invite. You have a beautiful home, Mr. O'Reagan."

"Please, it's Michael."

We're all waiting for Darragh, but when Mary enters and places plates in front of us, I look to Liam. I don't know why.

"Where is Darragh?"

"Darragh has gone away for a while," Liam says, looking at Finn before facing me and finally Father. Una seems to be frozen beside me.

"Gone where?" I ask, and from the look on Finn's face, this is news to him as well. My attention goes to Liam.

"What happened?"

"Please, we have two ladies at the table. Can we just have this meal?"

No, we fucking can't. Now all I can think of is the dead girl. Does this have something to do with Darragh's disappearance? Liam is eating his dinner, and Finn is too, along with Siobhan.

"I'll tell you later," Una whispers to me, and I steal a glance at her. She knows? So it couldn't be about the dead girl. That makes me breathe a little easier, and I give her a nod. She squeezes my leg under the table, and I suppress a smile.

"So you two are a thing?"

My attention snaps to Finn who is smiling at me, delighted at how uncomfortable things at the table just became. "Yes, we are."

Siobhan gives a big smile, and I nod at her in response before turning to Una, who has an eyebrow raised.

"We are?" I ask.

Una tilts her head while smiling. "Yes, we are." I want to kiss her, but everyone is staring at us.

Dad is waiting for me to explain, but I cut into my chicken. I ignore a kick under the table from Una and grin as I continue to eat. Her heavy sigh has my lips tugging.

"Michael, I hope you're okay with this." Una's voice is so sweet, and I take a quick glance at Father.

"Are you happy?" he asks her, and she doesn't hesitate, much to my delight.

"Very."

"Well, then it's okay."

His blessing does mean a lot, and when I glance to Una and see the happiness on her face, I know it means a lot to her too.

I surprise her when I place a gentle kiss on her lips. Her cheeks turn pink, but she's still smiling. A snigger from Finn has me returning to my food, but I can't get rid of the stupid grin I'm wearing.

The conversation flows easily around the table as the two girls chat about movies. I knew Una loved watching movies with Connor, but I didn't know she was still into them.

Her biggest love seems to be Denzel Washington. "I cry every time," Una tells Siobhan, who's nodding.

"Me too," Siobhan responds. It looks like a friendship is blossoming.

"But if you saw it already, why would you cry?" I ask once Mary has set out the dessert, tea, and coffees.

"He dies for her," Una says like I'm stupid. I love her feistiness.

"Yeah, but you already know that." I seriously can't understand this.

"It's just Denzel's acting," Siobhan interjects and Una agrees. It's fun at the table. It's different. The only person not taking part is Liam, but that's not unusual. What is unusual is how distant he's being. His mind isn't here, and that makes me think of Darragh.

"I think the girls make a great point." This is the first time Father has spoken through the meal. He's nodded and smiled, but he hasn't spoken.

"The kidnappers didn't do their homework. If they did, they would have never taken that girl. Denzel does a superb job. There are people in life that you shouldn't hurt." I glance toward Liam, but he's focused on Dad.

"It's like the most recent news," Dad says, putting down his spoon. "A young Northern Ireland boy, I think connected to the IRA, is missing, presumed dead. Whoever made the mistake of hurting him has messed with the wrong people." Silence fills the dining table, and I remind myself that he doesn't know.

"Oh, that would make a great film." Una's words are like water on flames, and she jumps right into a film about the IRA she saw and was disappointed in. I'm not sure if she's aware of what she's doing, but Father isn't finished, not by a long shot.

"Does the IRA kill the man's family for hurting one of their own?" he asks. I clench my jaw.

"I don't think so." Una shakes her head. She's really thinking about it. "No. No, they don't," she answers with more certainty.

"In real life, they would." Dad smiles after that before returning to his food.

"I didn't hear about that," I say, then I take a drink of tea. Liam and Dad are observing me way too closely, but I make my mind go blank.

"I did hear about the house that burned down in Kells," Liam says. That causes a flicker of fear to ignite in me.

"What happened? I hope no one was hurt," Una says, her voice kind.

"My friend, who works with me in Cavan, lives there in Black Water Heights," Liam explains. "She said no one was hurt, but the house burned right to the ground. The houses on either side didn't survive either. But thankfully, no one was hurt."

Una is frozen beside me, and my eyes snap to Liam, who doesn't seem to give a shit.

"I wonder what caused the fire?" I ask Liam.

"A cigarette not put out, faulty wiring, cooker left on… The list is truly endless."

I'm trying not to snap at him. Glancing at Una, I see she's as white as a fucking ghost. She's putting two and two together.

"Are you alright, Una?" Dad's hand covers hers, and I want to rip it off her. His patronizing words grate on me.

"Why wouldn't she be?" I snap, and silence fills the room.

"Shane." Una's surprise at me raising my voice has me reeling in my irritation. "I think I need some fresh air," she tells Father, and he smiles at her.

"How about a swim?" This suggestion comes from Finn, and Siobhan nods beside him.

"I don't have a swimsuit," Siobhan says with disappointment.

"I don't mind," Finn says, and she nudges him with her elbow.

"I can give you one," Una says. "And a swim actually sounds good." I'm surprised she spoke, and she looks up at me with such an innocent look on her face. "Are you coming?"

"You go ahead with Finn and Siobhan. I'll catch up," I tell her.

She hides her disappointment well before giving me a kiss on the cheek.

Once Finn, Siobhan, and Una leave, I ask about Darragh.

"He's in rehab," Liam explains. "Where he should have been a long time ago."

I agree with that assessment, if it's true.

"I have work to do." Dad stands now, his focus on Liam. He ignores me as he leaves. Angry, I suppose, that I raised my voice.

"You burnt the house down?" I ask the moment Father is gone. Liam pushes his chair out slightly from the table.

"Darragh left a cigarette lit."

I'm not buying it. He didn't know that I found the body, but I don't say anything about it. It's small compared to the other topic that Father brought up.

"Any idea who this boy is that Father was talking about?" I place my elbows on the table. I'm observing Liam for any signs that he knows.

"No, but it sounded like he was asking us."

I nod. That's exactly what it sounded like.

"Do you know who the boy is?" The question is delivered with a slight raised eyebrow. He thinks I'm involved, but he's grasping at straws.

"No, not a clue," I lie.

CHAPTER TWENTY-FIVE

O'REAGAN
AN CHLANN

UNA

I'm glad when Finn suggests swimming. Really, I would have grabbed any excuse to get out of that room. After coming back from my dad's grave and having a shower, telling Shane about Liam and my mother wouldn't help anyone.

It would cause more rows and more hate. I hope that Liam took my silence as a peace offering. I 'll find out in time if he accepted it or not.

Siobhan comes out of the bathroom of the pool house in the red bikini I gave her, and she looks like a sun-kissed goddess.

Her tanned skin seems to glow. Brown eyes smile at Finn as he appreciates each step she takes toward the pool. She's beautiful. Finn's very handsome. All the O'Reagans are. Too much, at times. Growing up around such stunning men had my expectations for the real world set too high. I think that's why I spent far too much time alone. Coming here in the summer was spent swooning over Shane. To think we're together now is crazy.

"What are you smiling at?" Siobhan asks me as she swims over to the side where I relax.

"Shane," I admit, and it's nice to say it out loud to another girl.

"I'm not going to lie. He scares me." Siobhan's voice is still light as she confesses how she feels.

"Liam scares me, but I get why Shane would."

"Liam is strange," Siobhan adds with narrowed eyes, and I laugh.

"Finn's a great guy."

"I can hear you," Finn says as he comes out of the changing room in a pair of white long shorts that ride low on his hips. He's all abs and wide shoulders, and Siobhan drinks him up.

I'd roll my eyes, but I can imagine that's how I view Shane too. Ducking under the water is nice. The water temperature is warm, but still, the initial sensation of being covered sends a shiver through me. After breaking the surface, I push my wet hair out of my face. Siobhan is swimming while Finn relaxes along the edge. I swim over to him.

"Did you know about Darragh?" I ask, treading water.

"No. I can't believe he's gone to rehab." Finn's face grows serious, and he scratches his brow. "It was sudden, because I'm sure I saw him this morning."

"Well, he's in the best place, I suppose." I move to the side of the pool and face out toward the large windows.

"When was the last time you saw him?" Finn asks, and I pretend to consider his question.

"Yesterday, I think," I tell him with a nod. "What do you think about your dad saying that about the Northern Ireland boy?" My question, I think, sounded simple, but Finn looks at me differently now as he moves around to face the window too. Glancing over my shoulder, I see the red bikini down the far end of the pool.

"I don't think anything about it. Why do you ask? You know something?" The suspicion is growing in his voice and the way he stares at me.

"I thought it weird, that's all," I answer while giving him a nudge, and he grins.

"You're starting to sound like one of us."

Flicking water at him, I laugh. "Shane is rubbing off on me," I say, and even as Finn laughs at me, I can see the question in his eyes. He's wondering what I really know.

For me, I can't help but think Michael was asking his sons, and it was last night that Shane had killed someone. Instead of letting the fear fester, I dive under the water.

Swimming relieves some tension that had been building inside me. Today was crazy, but chatting with Siobhan makes me feel normal. I'm not sure she could ever understand what her presence does for me. This big house with so much time on my hands can drive me a little crazy.

"Anyone want a drink?" Finn asks, climbing out of the pool. Siobhan takes the moment to admire him as water streams off his body, and he pulls his white shorts a bit lower.

"Yeah," I answer, and she looks at me over her shoulder and grins.

"Me too," she tells Finn.

We both get into the Jacuzzi. The water, at first, is almost too hot, but as I close my eyes, my whole body relaxes. "I so need this," I say.

"Me too. Finn's been so stressed lately." I open my eyes and look at Siobhan. "Over what?" I ask.

She pushes the water away from her with a delicate arm. "His brother."

I can't stop the snort that leaves my mouth. "Which one?" I ask, and she laughs.

"Yeah, I know. It's normally Darragh, but lately it's Connor. Who I have never met. I assume you have."

A fist tightens inside my belly. "Yeah, Connor's cool. He comes across a bit dark, but he's cool." Connor always reminded me of the Incredible Hulk. He was bigger than the other boys, and he was a force to be reckoned with. Anyone who stood in his way fell, and they fell hard.

"He misses him so much," she adds, and all I can do is nod.

The day I left my job, I drove to the cross guns for a few quiet drinks. It was there that I met Connor after three years of not seeing each other. We laughed a lot, and it was like old times. He made me promise that I wouldn't tell anyone, and I haven't. It hasn't crossed my mind, but right now, I question if telling Finn where Connor is would ease his mind. Finn arrives back with the drinks.

"I turn my back, and you girls are lapping it up," he says, handing me a bottle of Budweiser. Siobhan gets hers delivered with a kiss.

I look away even as I smile. It's nice to see Finn happy and see him with something that's his alone and not his and Darragh's.

When I finish my drink, I leave Siobhan and Finn alone. He's sitting closer to her, and I can see it in their eyes that they need some alone time.

I pull on a dressing gown and flip-flops as I make my way across the courtyard. It's cold outside, but after the heat of the pool house, I'm not surprised.

I pause at the door when I find Shane lying on the bed, his arm covering his eyes. Moving to him slowly, I notice the soft rise and fall of his chest. He's asleep. I need to get into dry clothes. The strap of my dressing gown is pulled, and I can't stop my heart from tripping as I turn to Shane. His eyes are open and focused on me.

"Did you have a nice swim?" he asks, pulling me closer while he sits up.

"I did," I tell him with a smile.

"Finn got to see you in a swimsuit before me?"

Finn's eyes were focused on Siobhan, and she was beach ready. My emerald green one-piece, along with my pale skin and red hair, isn't on the most desired list.

"You had your chance," I tease as he opens the belt of my dressing gown. I don't know why it's odd, but a nervous energy zings up my spine with the idea of him seeing me, yet I don't stop him. When he has it open, his warm hands go to my hips, and I shiver at the contact.

"A good job I didn't go swimming."

Holding my breath, I fear the worst.

"I don't think we would have done much swimming."

And like that, all my worries and insecurities fly away.

My body fits perfectly onto his lap. He doesn't complain about the cold water against his skin, and the contrast of his hot body has me pushing myself closer to him. Being this close to Shane allows me to see the strain around his eyes. Dark circles ring them. My lips press against each eyelid before I kiss his nose.

"As nice as this is, I need to have a shower and warm up," I tell him, leaving one final kiss on his lips. It's hard to walk away, but I need to warm up. The shower looks nice, but the bath is what calls to me.

I strip off as I pour in a bubble bath and run the taps. It doesn't take long for the room to fill with steam. Stepping into the bath, I lie back and close my eyes.

"I've changed my mind," I call out to Shane, in case he's waiting for me. "I'm taking a bath." Colors move from behind my eyes.

"I can see that." Water sloshes over the tub and onto the floor. I open my eyes and then narrow them at Shane.

"You nearly gave me a heart attack."

He's kneeling down along the side, his arm resting on the lip of the tub. He must have gotten wet, but he doesn't seem to care.

"I want to tell you a secret." I settle down as Shane speaks and rest my head against the back of the tub again. "You're not scary when you're mad. You're sexy as hell." I want to be offended, but his words send a thrill through my body.

"I can be scary," I tell him.

"Never," he tells me. His fingers dip into the water. He grazes my arm with his fingertips, and the sensation has a heartbeat thrilling in between my legs. I focus on his arm, his tattoo that always captures my attention.

"What does it mean?" I ask before gathering a pile of bubbles in my palm and blowing them toward Shane. He swipes them away quickly with a grin.

"My tattoo?" he asks, and there's uncertainty there. He isn't looking at me now.

"If it's private, you don't have to tell me."

"It's not that it's private. I just don't think it would do you much good knowing."

Now I want to know. I try to pull myself up in the bath, but Shane's fingers hold on to my arm. "I want to know who I'm lying beside," I say.

He laughs at my words, but his laugh is so tired and drained that my stomach churns with guilt at pushing him. But I hate not knowing every part of him.

"Okay, I'm going to tell you. But—and I mean it—no questions. No names. I'll tell you what it represents."

Why is my heart pounding? I nod my head. Shane holds my eye, and that gives me confidence that what the tattoos mean can't be so bad.

"For every death that I experience, I get a band added." My eyes are counting the bands rapidly, and Shane moves his arms.

"Una," he warns.

"I'm only counting them," I tell him, but I know that's not enough. Who died? Is one for his mum? The man who isn't okay from the other night? But no new ink covers his arm. The atmosphere becomes somber as I think of the man, the one who has been spinning around in my head.

"The missing boy from the North. Is he the same person as the man from the other night?"

There's a wild look of panic in Shane's eyes, but when he closes them and looks back at me, it's gone. "No, and don't ever let anyone hear you say that." He's taken my face in his hands, his words soft, and I nod.

"I won't," I tell him.

He relaxes back down along the side of the bath. We're both silent. I'm studying him as he stares at the water, and there's such a sadness there that my heart hurts. It's funny to feel such pain for someone else.

"What's bothering you?" I ask him, thinking there's no way he'll actually tell me. But I can ask. His gaze flickers up to me, and he reminds me of a cute puppy with his big brown eyes.

He exhales heavily before speaking. "Connor. I can't find him, and we need him home." I look away from Shane. I promised Connor I wouldn't say anything, but that was before.

"If you knew where he was, what would you do?"

Shane tilts his head and sits up a bit straighter. "I'd ask him to come home. We need him."

"Did he run away?" I ask.

"No. Una, do you know something?"

"I know where Connor is," I tell him, and his eyes widen like it's a miracle. Laughter bubbles up from his throat, confusing me, but when he looks at me, the light in his eyes has me smiling.

"I've been searching for him for a while. Is he far away?" Now that Shane is looking happier, I can use this to my advantage.

"The information will come at a price," I tell him with a smirk. I squeal as Shane jumps into the bath fully clothed. I think most of the water is now on the floor, but I can't stop the laughter.

"What the hell, Shane," I say, but he's moving over me, his lips getting closer.

"Name your price," he tells me, not an inch from my lips.

"You," I tell him, and he pays in full.

CHAPTER TWENTY-SIX

O'REAGAN
AN CHLANN

SHANE

I'm lying, gazing at her as she sleeps, and it's more beautiful now being this close. How many years have I watched her from the shadows? Her long stretches are pulling the quilt down slightly, showcasing the curve of her breast through her silky cream-colored, nightdress.

The desire to see her eyes has me running my fingers along her jawline. She stirs under my touch. Her lids half-open, and a goofy smile coats her face. "Good morning," she tells me, becoming more alert.

"*Is breá liom tú.*" I tell her I love her before kissing her puffy pink lips.

"*Tá mé i ngrá leat freisin.*" Her words have me smiling.

"I didn't know you spoke Irish so well."

She leans in and kisses my arm. "It's a phrase I know well, along with *póg mo thóin.*" Now she's giggling, and I can't help pulling back the covers and doing what she asked—kissing her perfect arse.

She's still giggling when I come back up and kiss her. "I have a surprise for you today," I tell her, but I'm nervous. Today, I want her to see Deerpark Stud Farm with me. I hope she loves it as much as I do.

"What should I wear?" Always such a dilemma for a woman. But with Una, she could wear anything.

"Be comfortable and wear whatever you want," I tell her with a final kiss before getting out of bed. She's still smiling as she gets dressed, and I can't stop myself from stealing kisses as we make our way down to breakfast. Mary has pancakes ready as I had requested the night before.

"Thank you, Mary," I say, and she looks at me twice. I hear "You're welcome" as we sit down.

"I'm going to get fat with all these pancakes," Una warns. The navy-and-cream sleeveless swing dress she's wearing makes her look sexy yet innocent.

"Even fat, you would be adorable," I tell her as Mary places the pancakes in front of us.

I've taken the Cadillac again today, knowing that it's Una's favorite. She's rubbing it and making small noises as she checks it out, and I'm afraid at how perfect everything is with her. I'm waiting for the other shoe to fall, always pessimistic. I push the darkness aside and steal glances of Una. Her smile is infectious, and I find myself grinning now and then.

"So where are we going?"

She's asked several times, and we're almost there. "Patience," I tell her, and she sticks out her tongue. If I wasn't driving, I know what I would do with it.

Pulling up at the large steel gates, I ring the bell, and a voice speaks out from the intercom. "Welcome to Deerpark Stud. Do you have an appointment?"

I flicker a quick look at Una, and her eyes dart to the large gates with the horse heads on them and then back to the monitor.

"Shane O'Reagan. I have an appointment." It takes a moment before the gates start to open.

"Please, come on in." I wait until the gates have fully opened before I drive up slowly. I let the roof down, giving Una a panoramic view.

I want her to love it.

"Why do you have an appointment here?" she asks, but her eyes are roaming the well-groomed fields. The old outbuildings come into view; they've been restored. But the most stunning part is the house.

A two-story white house that's over 12,000 square feet. Not as big as home, but still decent. The grounds, buildings, and house are in perfect condition—move-in ready.

When I stop the car, the auctioneer greets me. "Mr. O'Reagan." Then he takes Una's hand and shakes it. Afterward, she places her hands behind her back, looking unsure. Taking her hand, I twine our fingers together.

"There have been two more views for this place. Take a look around, but I wouldn't take long making a bid."

I nod, not wanting to talk money in front of Una.

"What kind of money are we talking?" Una asks sweetly.

The auctioneer looks at me, and I give him a nod that I hope Una doesn't see.

"One point five million. But I would say bid two million, and the place will be yours."

Una stumbles, and I hold on to her hand tighter.

"I'll leave you both to it. You can find me in the foyer after." He leaves, and he's not even out of earshot before Una starts.

"Two million euro! Why are you looking at this place?"

"*We* are looking at this place," I tell her, making my intentions clear.

"We," she repeats, color rising in her cheeks, and I can't help but kiss her lightly.

"We will need our own place, and Summer would be happy here," I say. She looks unsure again, so I take both her hands. "It's an investment."

"A huge one that I can't help with."

"I know that. But you would help run the place. It's a profitable business," I tell her, and I can see her softening.

"Just two million, Shane." Her exhale ends on a laugh like she can't believe it.

"Look at the place and tell me what you think."

We walk, and I observe Una as she takes it all in. "It's perfect Shane. But I mean, it's your decision."

I squeeze her hand. "There is no more me. Only us," I tell her, and she looks so perplexed that I find myself kissing her again.

"Can you see yourself living here?" I ask her as we make our way around to the house.

"Yes." She sounds almost breathless as we stop and admire it.

"Can you see yourself having a family here?" As I say it, my heart beats a little faster. It's something I've never thought about—something I never thought I would have. My own family. Una turns to me, her eyes searching my face.

"Yes." I kiss her deeply this time. "I love you," I tell her before we make our way into the house.

The auctioneer, as promised, is waiting in the foyer. The moment he sees us, he stands up. I let Una wander off as I speak to him. "I'll take it," I tell him.

"There will be other bidders," he starts.

Una looks happy here. That's all I need to know.

"Two million, and I want the deal closed by the end of the week," I tell him, and he's already getting his phone out to make the call.

After leaving Deerpark Stud, I take Una out for food in Cabra Castle. It's close to home and serves decent food. It's the first day in a long time that I can breathe. I know I still have a lot of problems, but they all seem easy to solve. Knowing where Connor is has made it all so much easier. Later tonight, I'll go get him, and his first job will be finding out what that girl Ava knows and keeping an eye on her. Brian will keep his mouth shut. If he doesn't, I won't touch him. I can get Connor to do that as well.

Moving the bodies is vital now. We need to clear out the bog. Leaving any form of evidence around isn't wise.

"You have to taste this pavlova. It's delicious." Una holds up a spoon to my lips filled with dessert. I take it and smile at her before breaking off a piece of my sticky toffee pudding and feeding it to her. She moans, and I think I'll keep doing this for a while.

"So you like the house?" I ask her in between spoonfuls. She nods and smiles. The auctioneer got back to me not long after leaving. The offer was accepted. The place is ours.

"Well, it's our new home." She stills for a moment, a piece of chocolate falling onto her chin. I reach across and clean it.

"Are you serious?"

I can't stop the smile. "Yes, I am," I tell her, and she squeals, getting the attention of an elderly couple beside us. She's around the table and in my arms quickly.

"I don't know what to say," she says with a look of awe on her face.

"You don't have to say anything. Just be my forever," I tell her and mean it. As long as I have Una, I'm stronger and better. Without her... I don't let that thought form.

"I've always been your forever." Her words send a thrill through me, and I kiss her lips softly.

Seal it with a kiss, I can almost hear my mother whisper. I do. I seal it all in, knowing it will always be there.

Get rest of the series and find even more book bundles by using the QR code below:

OTHER BOOKS BY VI CARTER

THE CELLS OF KALASHOV
THE COLLECTOR #1
THE SIXTH #2
THE HANDLER #3

MURPHY'S MAFIA MADE MEN
SINNER'S VOW #1
SAVAGE MARRIAGE #2
SCANDALOUS PLEDGE #3

SONS OF THE MAFIA
SINS OF THE MAFIA #0.5
VENGEANCE IN BLOOD # 1

YOUNG IRISH REBELS SERIES
MAFIA PRINCE #1
MAFIA KING #2
MAFIA GAMES #3
MAFIA BOSS #4
MAFIA SECRETS #5

THE BOYNE CLUB
DARK #1
DARKER # 2
DARKEST #3
PITCH BLACK #4

WILD IRISH SERIES

FATHER (PREQUEL)

VICIOUS #1

RECKLESS #2

RUTHLESS #3

FEARLESS #4

HEARTLESS #5

THE OBSESSED DUET

A DEADLY OBSESSION #1

A CRUEL CONFESSION #2

BROKEN PEOPLE DUET

BREAK ME #1

SAVE ME #2

ABOUT THE AUTHOR

Vi Carter - the queen of **DARK ROMANCE**, the mistress of suspense, and the high priestess of *PLOT TWISTS*!

When she's not busy crafting tales of the **MAFIA** that'll leave you on the edge of your seat, you can find her baking up a storm, exploring the gorgeous Irish countryside, or spending time with her three little girls.

Vi's Young Irish Rebels series has been praised by readers and can be found in English, Dutch, German, Audible and soon will be available in French.

And let's not forget her two greatest loves: ***coffee and chocolate***. If you ever need to bribe her, just offer up a mug of coffee and a slab of chocolate, and she'll be putty in your hands.

So, if you're ready to join Vi on a wild journey with the mafia, sign up for her newsletter and score a free book! Just be warned - her stories are so **ADDICTIVE**, you might not be able to put them down.

WHAT READERS ARE SAYING

Editorial Reviews

"Vi Carter has once again blown my mind with another outstanding story. She never fails to create a masterpiece with memorable characters that leap off the page. This book is complete perfection."- USA Today Bestselling Author Khardine Gray

Vi is one of those authors who never disappoints. She weaves **LOVE & DANGER** effortlessly. ★★★★★ stars

HOW TO KEEP IN TOUCH WITH VI CARTER

Visit Vi's website: https://author-vicarter.com/.

Join the newsletter: t.ly/yZWbX

Or scan the code below:

On Facebook, Instagram, TikTok and YouTube @ darkauthorvicarter and on Twitter @authorvicarter

Or scan the code below: